FA   ASTER

THE FALLING SERIES

SUSAN SCOTT SHELLEY

Copyright © 2020 by Susan Scott Shelley

Second Edition 2024.

This book is a work of fiction. Names, characters, places, and incidents are products of the author's imagination or are used fictitiously. Any resemblance to actual events, locales, or persons, living or dead, is entirely coincidental. This ebook is licensed for your personal enjoyment only. This ebook may not be re-sold or given away to other people. If you would like to share this book with another person, please purchase an additional copy for each person from proper authorized retail channels. Thank you for respecting the hard work of this author. All rights reserved, including the right to reproduce this book or portions thereof in any form whatsoever.

The publisher, Susan Scott Shelley, does not consent to any Artificial Intelligence (AI), generative AI, large language model, machine learning, chatbot, or other automated analysis, generative process, or replication program to produce, mimic, remix, summarize, or otherwise replicate any part of this novel, via any means: print, graphic, sculpture, multimedia, audio, or any other medium.

Cover photo used under licenses from Deposit Photos. Cover design is for illustrative purpose only, and any person(s) featured is a model.

FALLING FASTER

For Ty Allen, a trip to Los Angeles for a comic book collectors convention with his friends is the perfect place for the Buffalo based artist to hunt down rare issues for his collection, and take a much needed break. When he falls onto a display table, taking it down with him, and is saved from bodily injury by a man dressed as a popular comic book character, the trip takes an intriguing turn. One look into the dark eyes and sexy smile of the masked man with the lightning fast reflexes, and Ty wants to learn more.

Rock musician Craig Simms spends his spare time in a mask and a cape, bringing happiness to sick children in LA through his foundation. When he dives in to rescue Ty from a close call with the concrete floor, he ends up wrapped around the cutest guy he's ever seen. As they work together to clean up his wrecked display, he's drawn to Ty's friendly, sweet nature, and doesn't want their interaction to end.

A whirlwind weekend of chemistry and connection has them free-falling into something bigger than they'd anticipated. Ty is like a perfect melody for Craig's weary heart, and for Ty, Craig shifts every experience from muted tones to vibrant hues. But when the weekend is over and life takes new twists and turns, does what happens at the comic convention stay at the comic convention, or can they find a way to fit into each other's universes?

CHAPTER ONE
TY

Sounds come from every direction of the crowded convention center's vast hall. I flip through the row of colorful comic books, my gaze jumping between the issue numbers on the books and the numbers on the printed list I compiled.

Finding everything on my wish list is likely too much to hope for, even at the largest comic book collectors convention on the West Coast, but if I can score at least a few issues before the weekend is over, I'll consider the entire trip to LA well worth the cost of the plane tickets and hotel room fees.

The convention has drawn people from all areas of the country. Multiple accents mingle in the sea of people weaving around the grid pattern of vendors' tables. Aggressive, laser-focused seekers dodge and dart around those content to meander and explore every item they encounter.

I reach the end of the bin. Great issues, but nothing I need. Nodding at the vendor, I turn away from the table.

Groups of friends and families pass by, a reminder that I need to check in with my friends. Scanning the tables covered with comic books, memorabilia, artwork, clothing, and accessories, I spot Slater and Noah standing a few vendors away. My bag tucked tight against my side, I make my way over.

Having them along for the trip has eliminated the loneliness that usually accompanies my forays to various cities for conventions, but the couple's frequent PDAs are a tough reminder of my solo relationship status.

"Ty!" Slater's red T-shirt emblazoned with a lightning bolt stretching across his muscular chest rivals the brightness of his ginger hair. He holds up a comic book in a protective bag like it's a trophy and a triumphant grin lights up his face. "Look what I found."

"No way." I recognize the rare edition's yellow and green cover at first glance. That issue is one of the most coveted of those missing from my own collection. A thin blade of envy twists in my gut, but I smile and focus on happiness for my friend. "Want to discuss a trade?"

Slater's eyes bulge for a moment before he laughs and shakes his head. "Are you kidding? I've been looking for this issue for years."

"Same." I roll my shoulders and shrug away the disappointment. The convention still has two and a half days to go. Plenty of time left in my quest to find a hidden gem like one of the other rare comic books on my list. And if I don't have any luck by Sunday afternoon, I'll drown my sorrows by buying something fun and impractical like the life-size replica of Thor's hammer gleaming on the table to my left.

Noah slings his arm around Slater's waist, the tattoos decorating his biceps and forearms are on display thanks to his short sleeves. "Sorry, Ty. The guy who sold it to me said it was the only copy he had. No idea if he was bluffing though. I didn't know you wanted it too. We can go back to see if there's another one."

"I doubt he'd have another, but I'll check out his table

anyway. Maybe he'll have something else I need. I haven't made it anywhere near that side of the room yet."

"Did you find anything on your list?"

Shaking my head, I pull the sketchbook from my bag and then flip through the pages. "I got an idea for the project Slater and I are doing and wanted to get it down, so I spent most of the past hour sketching. Have a look."

The project, a collaboration sparked by Slater's idea for a comic book series about a hockey player who gains super powers, has taken over most of my free time for the last few months, as he and I take advantage of his hockey league's summer break. Most of our sessions, held at Slater and Noah's place, end with me stumbling to their guest room at the end of a late night. At this point, I feel like their extra, sometimes absent, roommate.

Noah's eyes widen as he scans the sketch. "You did all of that in the hour since we last saw you? Damn, you're talented."

A flush creeps into my cheeks. "Thanks."

Slater leans down and peers at the page. "I love it. The clashing of the hero and villain facing off on the ice would be a great scene to start off the next issue."

"I thought that too." Thinking along the same lines has worked well for our plans for the series.

He holds up his hand for a high-five. "Awesome."

I raise mine in response and overshoot the connection, my palm passing by Slater's. Laughter stealing my breath, I shrug at my friend and hold up my hand to try again. This time, I keep still and let Slater do the action. We connect with a *clap*.

From his place in the middle of our trio, Noah lays his hands on both of our shoulders. "That *has* to go into the story. One of your superheroes could be a little uncoordinated. Think of how funny you could make things."

My inspiration sparked, I nod at Noah and then jot down ideas on a fresh page. "A little uncoordinated, or we could go bigger and make him a walking disaster. A little like me. Crashing into things—"

"And flying into things," Slater adds, his blue eyes shining. "You aren't a walking disaster, Ty, but we could embellish some of the things that have happened to you. It's going to be so good. Great idea, Noah."

"I'm glad I thought of it. You guys have been working on the stories non-stop, and I've felt bad not having anything to contribute to help." Noah scuffs the toe of his sneaker on the concrete floor. He often spends the hours while Slater and I work, close by, lost in a book. The man is a voracious reader. "I feel like I'm out of my element when you're both hardcore into planning worlds and characters."

Slater bends his head and kisses Noah on the temple. "Just having your support means everything to me. Both with the series and with being here now. I know this convention isn't your thing or your idea of a mini-vacation, but I'm glad you're here."

Love shines bright in Noah's eyes as he leans into his boyfriend's side. "Are you kidding? I'm loving watching you get so excited over everything here."

Their lips meet in a brief kiss and something deep within me aches to find that level of love. The two of them together are sweet. Besides being boyfriends, they are best friends, roommates, and teammates on Buffalo's pro hockey team, the Bedlam.

Unable to ignore the stab of loneliness, I flip the sketchbook closed. Work has consumed all of my time. Maybe when we return home, I can steal some hours from my schedule and try to get back out there and meet someone new.

Noah turns to me and swings a friendly arm around my

shoulder. "Come on, we'll help you find one of the books on your list."

"Thanks. I appreciate having a second, or I guess third, set of eyes and hands to check." I fall in step beside Noah and allow Slater to lead the way.

In the six months I've been friends with the couple, I've appreciated how they always look out for me. I met Slater first, at a bar when we were both nursing broken hearts and we bonded over a shared love of comic books. Lucky for Slater, he and Noah worked out their problems. And lucky for me, I gained two supportive friends.

After a few unsuccessful stops at tables, we wind our way to the far side of the room. Large sponsor logos line the wall, interspersed with larger-than-life cut-outs of superhero figures, and the foot traffic isn't as heavy as it is in the rest of the convention.

Slater pauses under a giant vinyl banner with the convention's name. "We need to get a selfie with this. Come on."

Used to his penchant for photos and social media, I crowd in close to the pair and grin at the image the three of us make on Slater's phone. "I want a copy of this."

"Sure." Slater tugs Noah against his side and they place me in the center of the shot. He takes a few photos, and as we part, his fingers tap away on his screen. Seconds later, my phone vibrates with the new messages.

Murmuring my thanks, I hold out my hand, indicating I want Slater's cell. "I'll play photographer. Let me get a wider range shot of you and Noah, so you get the whole banner in the background."

My gaze on the pair through the camera's lens, I back up several steps. Something solid smacks into my foot and lower leg, knocking my feet from under me. Arms flailing, I fall backward, fear flipping through my stomach. I catch the expressions of horror on Slater and Noah's faces and their dash toward me. Too late to help.

My back slams into a hard and unyielding surface and it tips backward, taking me along. Breath catches in my lungs. The ceiling rushes by amid the sounds of chairs scraping the ground and footsteps pounding. My meeting with the concrete floor is imminent. Legs in the air, I tuck my chin to my chest and cradle my head with my arms. A storm of colorful pamphlets rains around me.

Bracing for impact, I wish I embodied any one of the superhero powers I've given my characters.

"I've got you," a deep voice calls.

The swish of a dark cape obscures my vision. Strong arms wrap around me, and a hard body softens my landing.

We slam into the floor. My back bows and I wince at the pull in my muscles. The stranger's hold ensures that my head stays safely away from the unforgiving concrete. I lay, gasping for breath, heartbeat galloping away strong enough that the stranger can probably feel it through his gloves.

"You okay?" That deep voice speaks again. The cape slides away from my face, but those strong arms stay around me.

"Yeah, thanks. Are *you*?" I crane my neck. The only bits of him I can see are black pants and gloves.

Slater jumps over the upended table and lands in a crouch at my side. "Ty! Are you okay?"

"I think so." I grasp hold of his extended hands. As Slater pulls, I attempt to get my legs under myself, and push the rest of the way to standing.

Next to Slater, Noah reaches to help my rescuer.

Readying my thanks, I turn.

And stare.

My mouth falls open.

"No freaking way." Dropping to my knees, I hold out my hand to assist in hauling the man from the floor. The guy's Batman costume looks like a top of the line model. I'd briefly priced those last Halloween before learning that my ex had no intention of joining me at the comic book store's party. I went alone as the Joker. "Um, wow. Dude, thanks for saving me."

Brown eyes as warm as whiskey peer at me from behind the mask. A smile curves lips marred by a scar that runs from his lower lip to the cleft in his chin. "Anytime."

Our hands meet and clasp, and together with Noah's help, we pull the guy to standing.

"I…" I drag my gaze away and survey the damage I've caused.

In addition to the upended table and what appears to be hundreds of pamphlets covering the floor, I knocked over posters, two life-sized superhero cutouts, and a tablet.

Embarrassment covers me like a heavy blanket. Heat flushing through my body, I rake a hand through my hair and blow out a breath. "I'm sorry. I'll help clean it all up."

"Hurricane Ty strikes again." Smiling, Slater rights the table as though it weighs nothing and heaving the large object costs him zero effort.

I take the two steps to close the distance between myself and the stranger. "As my buddy said, I'm Ty. Did you get hurt?"

"Craig. And I'm fine." Craig clasps my hand again, encasing me in soft leather and a secure grip. "I think you tripped over one of my boxes, so what happened was my fault. It must have gotten pushed out from beneath the table."

I have to tilt my head back a bit to meet Craig's gaze, which puts the man somewhere in the six-one or six-two range. Craig smiles again, and sparks of attraction tingle through my blood. I want the mask gone so I can see all of

Craig, uninterrupted. "I should've been watching where I was going."

"Let's call it even."

I nod and as I hold Craig's gaze, an electric thrill shoots through me, hot and lightning fast. The world around me dims to Craig and then to the strong fingers holding mine tight.

A shout sounds from somewhere behind me and the world flares into brighter focus. Sounds and scents creep in along with the realization that he and I are still joined together, and we have an audience. I force myself to release my hold. Muscles quivering, I stagger a step and then bang into Slater. Either Craig has dazzled me or I'm still feeling the surge of adrenaline from my fall. "Uh, these are my friends Slater and Noah."

As the guys shake hands, I crouch and begin gathering pamphlets. They advertise a foundation that sends volunteers dressed as superheroes to visit sick children in hospitals, houses for those bound to home care, and other charitable endeavors. And Craig, in his costume, is right there in the center of the picture.

Damn it.

I feel even worse.

"Um, Ty." Slater's hesitant voice pulls my attention.

I glance to my left, then to Slater lifting my sketchbook from a puddle of coffee.

"No." Horror and panic flashing like strobe lights, I rush to the book. My bag, which had slipped off my shoulder during the fall, is open. Beside it, a to-go coffee cup is on its side in a pool of tan liquid.

Dread increasing, I take the book from my friend's hands. Coffee drips from the pages. Helplessness wells as I sink to my knees, searching for something to wipe off the mess and stop further damage. I don't spy anything aside from my canvas bag, which wouldn't be a smart idea.

"I'll grab paper towels from the restroom," Noah calls, sprinting away.

Nodding, I leaf through the book to assess the damage. Parts of sketches have bled. Pages are sticking together. Hours of work, gone. I press my hand to my forehead. "Come on, no."

Craig crouches beside me. The warmth of his hand seeps into my shoulder. "I'm sorry. Is any of it salvageable? It seems I owe you a sketchbook. That was my coffee."

I sit back on my heels and fight through the tangle of feelings, forcing myself to focus on the positive, not the negative. Everything can be drawn again. It will take ages, but can be done. I'm lucky the entire book hasn't been ruined. Most lucky of all is that neither Craig nor I had been hurt during the fall. "It'll be okay. I owe you a coffee."

The sound of sneakers pounding over concrete announces Noah's return. He thrusts a wad of towels at me. "Here."

"Thanks." The rough, folded papers are thin and coffee soaks through faster than I can change them. Craig joins in, passing me towels and helping to wipe the book's exterior. Murmuring my thanks, I begin the task of layering the towels between the stained pages, careful not to tear any of the weakened sheets.

His heated touch lands on my shoulder once more, but is gone in the span of a heartbeat. "You worry about saving what you can of your book. I'll get the rest of the coffee."

Craig mops up the coffee in between handing me extra towels. Slater and Noah are slowly straightening the mess around us. Guilt over my friends restoring order to the chaos I've caused hits hard and fast. I owe them at least a drink for their trouble. With the last of the paper towels, I line the bottom of my bag, in case any drips work their way out of the dampened pages, then tuck the book inside. "Craig, I'm sorry about all of this. I can be a walking disaster."

"Hence, the nickname." Slater props one of the cutouts at the far end of the table. "But we love you, Ty."

Craig once again extends his hand and helps me to my feet. His glittering gaze and small smile invite me to play. "Then I guess you might need a superhero around all the time?"

"I wouldn't turn one away." That spark of attraction flashes bright. Craig's fingers tighten for a moment before he lets go of my hand. Blowing out a breath, I force myself to focus on the mess, not on flirting. I glance at my T-shirt and jeans. No coffee splashes, thank goodness.

We gather the rest of the pamphlets and I straighten the stacks of glossy paper until they are perfectly aligned, working side by side with Craig while Slater and Noah capture wayward papers that drifted into the foot traffic.

When everything is back in its proper place, I glance at Craig, not ready to say goodbye. "All done. It's like I was never here. Sorry again that I was a human wrecking ball."

"I'm not. Ending up with you in my arms was the best thing I've had happen in a long time." Craig takes a step closer, closing the distance between us. The intensity and interest in the gaze raking over my face sets off twin buzzes of hope and desire. "If you're not busy…"

"Yes?" Quick and eager, the response bursts from my lips. I don't care if my friends give me a hard time for having zero game later, as long as Craig's next words are something that keeps me in the man's company.

Craig gestures at the display table. "I'm finished my shift here. And I'd like to make up for your sketchbook. Can I offer you a ride in a replica of the Batmobile? It's parked outside."

From the way he lowered his voice, I figure the offer isn't one he extends easily or often. My excitement level soaring, I force my voice to match the same hushed tone. "Are you kidding? You drive a replica of the Batmobile?"

"It's not mine. It belongs to the foundation. Whoever is dressed as Batman drives it when visiting the kids or doing appearances. The car adds to the fantasy. You should see how excited the kids get. Makes me smile every single time." With a smile, he waves at someone behind me. "I have to return it to the foundation's headquarters. Come take a drive with me. My car's there so I can take you back to your hotel afterward."

"Um, yes, absolutely. I'm there." But then I think about my friends, and how much the experience would mean to Slater. "If you don't mind, I know Slater would love to see it, too."

"I would love to see what?" Slater walks up behind us, followed by Noah.

Craig turns toward Slater, his cape swooshing in the breeze from an overhead fan. "I have a replica of the Batmobile out back."

"Seriously?" Slater's eyes light up and his gaze bounces from Craig to the exit and back again. "And you're letting us see it? That's so awesome."

Noah slips an arm around Slater's waist. "You've made his year, Craig."

Excitement shifts to something softer and warmer as Slater shakes his head and gazes at Noah. "No. Noah, *you've* made my year, but yeah, Craig, this will be a close second."

Feigning indignation, I cross my arms over my chest and raise a brow. I can't help teasing Slater. "And what about me? Where do I fall in your list of hits for the year?"

"Um..." Slater pauses, and I can practically see the

wheels turning as he tries to figure out a diplomatic answer. "A tie for second, as my best new friend?"

Shaking my head, unable to keep my smile from showing, I shoulder my bag and then nudge Slater's arm. "I guess I'll take it."

Two people dressed as Black Panther and Captain Marvel arrive at the booth. Craig introduces them as his replacements and then explains that most of the foundation's volunteers will be taking a shift at the table during the convention.

"Ready?" Craig flashes me another smile.

"Definitely." I fall in step beside him. So many people stare at us as we walk through the crowded hall. I know that's due to his costume, but the man's presence is magnetic regardless. Behind us, Slater and Noah debate restaurants to try for dinner tonight. Craig asks which hotel we're staying in and offers suggestions of cafes and restaurants frequented by locals.

The heavy double doors of the exit come into view. Craig shoves one open and gestures for us to pass. Nodding my thanks for him holding the door, I slip by him. Bright, blinding sunlight greets us. Wincing, I shade my eyes and wait until he's by my side once more. The four of us fan out, walking in a line, and though there are people in the parking lots and sounds of traffic streaming from the roads, it's nowhere near the level of noise we experienced inside the convention center.

Tucked in a private parking area, the replica Batmobile gleams in the sunshine, black and sleek and amazing.

"It's…" My fingers itch to touch the car. I glance from the car to Craig and back again. "I don't even have words to describe it."

"I do." Voice hushed, Slater reverently runs a hand along the hood. "It's awesome."

The tips of Craig's fingers brush my skin from my biceps to my forearm, raising goosebumps in their wake. "You can touch it. Or get in. Whatever you want."

The spark from the contact zips right to my dick. For a moment, I hold still, gaze locked on Craig's warm brown eyes, suspended by the fireworks erupting through my system. When Craig lowers his hand and gestures to the car, I take a breath to get a hold of myself, open the door, and slide into the driver's seat.

The steering wheel's leather is smooth under my palms. I check out gadgets, gauges, and everything in the interior. "It's so cool. I can picture us zooming off to fight crime somewhere."

"Right?" Slater takes photo after photo, including selfies with Noah, Craig, and me. "You should start thinking about your superhero name."

Craig smiles and leans his hip on the hood. "I kind of like The Hurricane."

Phone in hand, Noah works his way around the car, pausing every few steps to take another photo. "Appropriate considering the levels of destruction they cause and Ty's love of the villains."

"Ha ha." But I grin and climb out of the car so Slater can have a turn in the driver's seat and I can take some photos of my own, including one of Noah leaning into the car kissing Slater. "You should get inside with Slater, Noah. That'll make a good picture."

He complies, rounding the car and climbing into the passenger seat. Slater puts his arm around Noah's shoulders and they both smile for me. I capture the image. Slater looks over the moon happy and Noah's eyes are filled with love as he watches Slater geek out over the sleek ride.

Noah pushes the car door open. "Don't worry, Ty, I got a

bunch with you sitting in here too. I'll send them to you later."

No matter how many times Noah and Slater have done considerate things, both little and big, I am continually surprised and never expect it. They are damn good friends, and I'm grateful for them. "I appreciate it."

"No problem."

Slater exits the car. "Thanks, Craig. Sitting in that is something I'll never forget."

"Want to go for a drive in it? We can take it around the parking lot." The way Craig's eyes are crinkling at the corners, he's definitely enjoying how much we're all savoring this experience.

Letting out a whoop, Slater rushes around to the passenger side of the car and grins at Noah and me. "I get to *ride* in the Batmobile. Someone pinch me. I better not be dreaming."

"I'll take a video," Noah promises as Craig climbs into the driver's seat. The engine roars to life and Slater waves, then blows Noah a kiss, which Noah returns. As I wave them off and Noah taps the video button to start recording, he glances at me. "Thanks for including us in this. You didn't have to do that."

"Are you kidding? I couldn't have just gone with Craig and not shared this with you guys. I knew how much this would mean to Slater."

He returns his focus to the screen and smiles at Slater grinning and chatting with Craig. "You don't even know how much. We found a place out here that does exotic car rentals and they actually have a replica just like this one, but it wasn't available this weekend. Slater was pretty bummed. So, him getting to experience this is really special."

I watch Craig's profile as the car zips around in a loop. I

can't wait to see him unmasked. "And it wouldn't have happened at all if I hadn't literally crashed into Craig's space today."

Still recording, Noah pulls his focus from the screen. His expression turns serious and he lays his other hand on my shoulder. "You shouldn't label yourself as a walking disaster, Ty. You beat yourself up too much."

The label has stuck for so long, I've had more years with it, than without. All I can do is shrug. You hear something enough, you begin assuming it's true. "I guess."

"You do. Way too hard on yourself. Besides, I think Craig likes you just as you are."

The car comes to a stop in front of us. Slater hops out, wearing a mile-wide grin. "All yours, Ty."

I take a moment to capture the image of Craig in the costume and the car in my mind. Things like this don't happen to me. Ever. With a heady rush of anticipation, I bid my friends goodbye and climb in.

Craig smiles and brushes a gloved finger along the back of my hand. "Ready to go?"

Body buzzing, I suck in a breath. "I'm ready for anything."

CHAPTER TWO
CRAIG

Sunlight dances through the clouds and drenches the street. I drive along roads dotted by palm trees, my attention captured by the long, lanky, blond man in faded jeans and a gray T-shirt with *Supervillain* written across the chest at my side. When I'd dived to save Ty from hitting his head on the concrete floor, something like electricity sparked from a place deep within me and crackled to life.

Ty grins, and his smile lights up his face. "Thank you so much for this. I can't get over that I'm driving with Batman in the Batmobile. But now I'm wishing I'd cosplayed as the Joker today. Imagine how fun that would look to the people watching us."

In addition to being the cutest guy I've seen in a long time, Ty is friendly and sweet. The attention he gave to putting the display to rights and how he invited his friends to see the car because it obviously would mean a lot to Slater shows that.

"The perfect couple." Offering the ride in the car had been an impulse decision, spurred by the desire to prolong our connection. But the best things in my life have all come from impulse decisions. Something tells me that Ty will be the same. I slow to a stop for a red light. "Tell me about yourself."

His rich brown gaze roams my face, settling on the scar at my chin before returning to meet my stare. "What do you want to know?"

"Everything. Let's start with something easy. I know you're staying at a hotel for the convention, but are you local? Where do you live?"

"Buffalo."

"New York?"

"Yeah."

Surprise tickles through me. "I grew up there."

He gapes at me. "Seriously? Small world. What part? I'm from East Amherst."

"South Buffalo." Maybe the universe is trying to tell me something. My last visit home, during Christmas, seems so long ago. "I still have family and friends there. I get back a few times a year."

"How long have you lived in LA?" Leaning his hand on the dashboard, Ty peers at the passing palm trees. His long fingers are a distraction. I can easily imagine them grasping a pencil as he brings an image to life on a sketchbook's page.

The light changes to green and I focus again on the road. "I've been out here for close to ten years."

Ty leans back in the seat and lifts his face to the sun. He closes his eyes, smiling as he soaks up the warmth, like he's immersing himself in the experience. "Do you like it? I've never lived anywhere other than Buffalo."

"I did for a while, but lately I'm thinking I might need a change."

"Change is good. I mean, not always, of course, but it can

be. And if you're feeling it in *here*," voice growing earnest, he lays his hand over his heart, "then you should do it."

His passionate statement hangs in the air. He obviously speaks from experience. I long to touch him, to soothe any roughened places that might still be tender. "Sounds like there's a story there. One I want to hear, but let's wait until we're out of the sweltering heat, and able to be face to face without any barriers between us."

In the corner of my vision, Ty shifts, angling his body in my direction. "What do you do when you're not in a mask and cape?"

Not quite ready to talk about my other career, I turned the car's fan up two notches. "I'm a musician. But the mask and cape gig is my favorite role. I love the way the kids and even their parents light up, excited and happy. It's an escape from the difficult situations they're going through, and being a part of that is really special."

Ty's eyes sparkle and his smile is like sunshine on a cloudy day. My breath catches at how brilliantly he shines. "That's how I feel about the world of comic books. Finding friendships in the fandom, being able to lose yourself within the colorful pages of a story, and characters that people identify with and see in themselves. That's what I want to draw and create and bring to other people."

"I didn't get to see much of the inside of your sketchbook, but I love the reason you want to create things." I pull into the foundation's parking lot. "We're here."

After parking in the private garage, I lead the way indoors. Ty and I take a quick tour of our floor, the bland cubicles and conference rooms brightened by large, colorful posters, then I leave him in the waiting room and head to the locker room so I can change out of the costume. Usually, I'm a little bummed when I have to slip out of a superhero suit, but today, I'm eager to shed it so I can get back to Ty.

Dressed in my regular clothes, I pause by the full length mirror and examine my reflection. Without the mask and cape, will Ty find me lacking, or will he like what he sees?

Nerves spill through me, not unlike the rush I get before every gig. Blowing out a breath, I rake a hand through my hair and then turn away from the mirror. Making my way through the hallways back to Ty, the urge to shove my hands in my pockets or play with the leather strap that encircles my wrist is strong, but I resist and force a facade of calm confidence.

Ty stands when I enter the room. His attention flies to my face and lingers, sparking a jolt to my system when our gazes collide, before journeying to my T-shirt, jeans, and sneakers, then up again. He saunters closer, smiling, and closes the distance between us. "I like your tattoo."

The nerves settle to a steady hum of anticipation. I glance at my left forearm. The tattoo of a rose and thorns interwoven with music notes wraps around my skin from my wrist to my elbow. I hold still as Ty traces a finger along the stem. The touch is like tiny sparks of electricity, a live wire that increases in intensity when Ty's chocolate gaze meets mine once again. I lick my dry lips. "I got it when I was eighteen. Creating music is beautiful, but it can be painful too."

Light comes into Ty's eyes and his fingers pause on my skin. "You said you were a musician. What do you play?"

"Guitar, piano, and the drums."

"So, what kind of musician are you? Are you in a band, a solo artist, or something else?"

My immediate thought is of Cody, Patrick, and Devon, my original bandmates and best friends. "I've been in several bands. Right now, I'm mainly a songwriter for other artists, but I play the occasional gig in friends' bands and I still create music with my original band. I moved out here with them, with dreams of being a rock star."

Ty trails his fingers back and forth along the sensitive line of skin. He is close enough for me to see the lighter shade of caramel in his eyes and to smell the fresh scent of his shampoo. Imagining that delicate, teasing touch on other parts of my body is too easy and too tempting. "I'm impressed. A superhero *and* a rock star. This is my lucky day."

The urge to touch Ty is too strong to ignore. I curl my fingers around the man's warm hand, locking us together. "I feel like the lucky one."

Ty's lips parted. He sucks in a breath and drops his focus to our hands, then takes a slow journey back to my face. "You don't know anything about me yet."

"Not true." I lift my free hand so I can tick off each thing I've learned on my fingers. "I know you were nice enough to stick around and help clean up the display table. And you're a good friend because you made sure your buddy wouldn't miss out on something that obviously meant a lot to him. When we were taking that lap around the parking lot, Slater also told me that you're helping him bring his comic book idea to life. And I know you're an artist from Buffalo. That's a good start."

Laughing, Ty nods. "All right." Then his gaze tracks to my other tattoo, peeking from beneath the shirtsleeve on my right bicep. "Can I look?"

I inwardly cringe, but raise my sleeve to reveal the smiling purple narwhal wearing a blue and yellow striped necktie.

Ty's brows shoot up, then narrow as he studies the ink. "Whoa. That's... not at *all* what I was expecting."

"Me either, when I woke up and found it on my arm."

With a grimace, I elaborate, "I got it after a show, years ago, on my first tour. I was drunk, wasted to the point that I don't remember anything after stumbling through the tattoo parlor's doors with my band. But I guess I asked for this, or one of the other guys talked me into it. No one could remember how it went down. They were all in the same state as me. And we all ended up with tats."

"The tattoo parlor shouldn't have given you anything when you were in that condition." The quiet words accompany a light flexing of his fingers under our joined hands.

"I agree. I don't like the tattoo and occasionally think about getting it removed or covered. For years while I toured, it was an effective reminder to never let myself get in that state again." Worry over what Ty is thinking rushes my words. "Not that I'm in that same place anymore. I'm not. That was all youth and stupidity and trying too hard to live up to an image. That night was the last time I let myself get in that condition. The tattoo was a wake up call I needed. I might make mistakes, but I try my best not to make them twice."

With a gentle smile, Ty strokes the narwhal's horn. "I think it's cute."

"I guess I can live with cute." Happiness warms through me like the sun's rays, bright and beaming as we smile at each other. Craving the feeling of that tempting mouth against my lips, I step the smallest bit closer, intent on eliminating the distance between us.

Ty raises his face, watching me, eyes heavy-lidded with desire. Then, in a blink, surprise skips over his features. His free hand latches on to my forearm and those long fingers curl into my skin. "Band? On tour? Wasted? You really *are* a rock star, aren't you?"

Discomfort at the label rolls through me. I shake my head.

"Not the star part so much. As I said, I've been in several bands. Some of them have had success. Others, not so much. But these days, I really am more of a songwriter. I play some shows here and there, and I still create music with my original bandmates, but I haven't lived the life of a touring musician in a few years."

"That's... wow. I don't know what to say. You're probably one of the most interesting people I've ever met." Ty releases his hold and steps back so we're no longer touching, but not so far that I couldn't reach out and hold him. He fidgets with the strap on his bag and his teeth sink into his lower lip. "My life is boring compared to yours."

"I sincerely doubt it." Wanting to ease his worry, I take a step closer, but voices carrying in from the hall are a reminder we're not alone. "Let's get out of here. We need to replace that sketchbook."

"Craig." Ty shifts his weight from one foot to the other. "Really, you don't have to do that."

"I insist. If someone spilled something all over my guitar, or my piano... Hell, I've spilled coffee and beer on lyrics I'm writing, so I know what it's like to have your tools messed with or ruined." I don't know if I'll ever be able to erase from my mind the disappointed, deflated look that had crossed Ty's face when he'd held the ruined sketchbook. "Let me do this."

Ty cocks his head to the side and, after a beat where I worry he'll say no, nods. Then he lifts his chin, crosses his arms over his chest, and raises a brow. "All right. But only if after we're done with that, I get to buy you a coffee to replace the one that spilled."

"Deal."

I'm treated to surprise skipping across Ty's features once again and a laugh sputters from his lips. "That was quick. I thought I'd have a fight on my hands."

The temptation to touch, to reassure, is too strong to ignore. In a few steps, I lay my hand over Ty's heart. It beats strong under my palm and his shirt is so soft, beckoning a caress. "I don't think you'd ever have to work hard to convince me to spend time with you."

The laugh and smile fade as Ty's eyes widen. He seems genuinely stunned. "Oh."

Would Ty wear the same expression after we've kissed? I'm sure his kiss will stagger me. "Let's go. Fair warning, my regular car isn't anywhere as cool."

"As long as it runs, that's all that matters."

Ty stays close as I lead the way outside. My black Corvette has over one hundred thousand miles, and has seen better days. I open the door for Ty, then hurry to climb in the other side. "There's an art supply store across the street from my favorite guitar shop."

As we drive, Ty tells me about the comic book series he and Slater are working on. The way he lights up in excitement and enthusiasm discussing something he loves, is beautiful.

In the store, strolling the aisles, I listen, enrapt as Ty teaches me about paper types and the uses of the different pencils, and points out the pros and cons of various mediums. The fascination has nothing to do with the items, although I'd been curious, and everything to do with the passionate, enthralling man himself. Ty is sparkling, like sunlight on water or a star shooting across the sky.

He selects a sketchbook nearly identical to the ruined one in his bag. I pay, then pocket the receipt, happy I now have knowledge of what he likes to work with.

We leave the store, and Ty pulls me toward a small cafe two shops down. "And now, coffee."

"Think I'll go with iced instead of hot."

"Me too. Slater laughs about how many sugars I use, but I like it sweet."

"I won't laugh," I promise.

Large coffees in hand, we settle at an outside table protected from the sun by a rainbow-striped umbrella. I wrap my hands around my cup, the welcome chill seeping into my skin. "What do you think you'll draw first in the new book?"

He tips his head as he swirls the ice in his drink. "Probably the scene I sketched this morning. It's one for the series with Slater."

"I'd love to see some of your art."

"I can make that happen. Hold on." Ty pulls out his phone, taps the screen a few times, then sets it in front of me. "Here. My portfolio."

Picture after picture reveals dozens of drawings of superheroes, fiery dragons, calm seascapes, mythological creatures, and portraits of several people. I recognize Slater and Noah among the group. "These are unreal. You're really talented."

"I've been drawing since I was a kid." His gaze turns thoughtful. "I never gave serious thought into making it into a career until a few years ago. My twenty-fifth birthday was an eye-opening, mini life crisis. Some family and friends were going through stuff that led me to question what I was doing with my life and what would it take to be happy. Art as a career was the answer."

I hand Ty the phone. "You should definitely be drawing."

He sets it on the table, then withdraws a pencil from his canvas bag along with the fresh sketchbook. The bag from the art supply store crinkles as he stuffs it into his bag. His gaze on my face, he taps the pencil against a blank page a few times, then begins making fast, faint lines, returning his scrutiny to me every few strokes. "I'm still working at a regular office job, handling home and auto insurance claims, but I shifted from full to part time last year. I wanted more time to spend on my art."

"Taking a leap and putting a plan into action is a huge thing. That's amazing."

"Not yet. But someday, it will be." His hand moves quickly over the page. I glimpse strands of wavy hair, similar to my own.

Metal scrapes over concrete as I move my chair beside Ty's to better view the artist in action. "You sound like someone who has plans."

"I do. Big dreams." Determination pours out of his posture and for a moment, his eyes glint with defiance aimed at the paper. Or more likely, a situation or someone who hadn't supported his dreams. "And I'll do whatever it takes to chase them."

I take a long pull of the sweetened brew. "Sounds like the change you mentioned earlier."

With a sigh, Ty stops sketching. He lifts his coffee to his mouth. The condensation on the outside of the cup drips over his fingers. "A lot has changed for me, compared to how things were a few years ago. Switching to part time meant I had to downsize a lot and cut back on things. Make sacrifices, some easy, some not. This is the first vacation I've taken in three years. Instead of having my own place, I'm sharing a house with two roommates."

"Slater and Noah?"

Ty shakes his head, smiles, and resumes sketching. "With how often I'm over there, it seems like I'm living with them, but no. I wish. My roommates are two guys who work odd hours and aren't interested in being friends. One uses up all the hot water when taking showers, and the other plays music at top volume and leaves stuff everywhere. Even so, I'm much happier than I used to be."

"Being happy is the most important thing." I lean back in my chair, watching my own likeness form on the page. Memories surface of my early days in LA. "I moved out here at eighteen with my three best friends, and money was so tight, we were scrounging for change, working whatever jobs we could around band practices and gigs. Bartender, bike messenger, you name it, I did it. All the sacrifices were worth it."

"Are your friends still here?"

"I wish. Only one out of the three. Cody's dad got sick early on and he went back home to help out. Devon followed two years later. Patrick, the last member of our group, is still here. He's a studio musician. We get together as often as we can. The last time the four of us were all together was back in Buffalo at Christmas. We recorded a few songs, had a great time doing it. Whenever we're all together, it's like no time has passed at all."

He bumps his knee against mine. "You sound a little wistful."

"I miss them, and how we all were together, but I guess we ended up where we were supposed to be." That's what I tell myself, but I wonder if it's true. Lately, I've been missing them more and more. Thinking about those early days and how much happier I was back then. Wishing they were still here. Maybe it's time for another trip back home.

Ty's pencil stills over the sketch and then he signs his name with a flourish and tears the page from the book. "Here."

I'm staring at myself, in shades of gray and white. It looks like me, but kinder maybe. And definitely happier. Is that how Ty sees me? "Wow. Can I keep it?"

The corners of Ty's lips lift into a smile. He looks up from sliding the supplies into his bag and nods. "Of course."

I tuck the paper under my sunglasses and keys so it won't blow away. A thrill skips through me when Ty's fingers brush along my hand. Not an accidental brush, but a deliberate, slow caress. Little strikes of lightning flare along my skin as the fingers flex and shift, exploring the back of my hand.

When they slip under to play against my palm and fingers, I tense, but Ty doesn't pause or recoil when he encounters the callouses on my fingertips, earned from years of playing guitar. The light touches raise more nerve endings in their wake. Aroused beyond anything I've dreamed from such soft contact, I suck in a breath, rotate my hand, and return the gentle grazes over Ty's talented fingers.

Lips parting, eyes heavy-lidded, expression full of yearning, Ty shifts closer. "Craig."

My pulse pounding with a steady beat of desire, I bend my head and close the distance, watching Ty's eyes darken, and breathe in the scent of coffee and the hint of mocha he added to his order. I pause, the scantest of spaces from Ty's mouth, savoring the anticipation. Every single thing about the man by my side is wonderful and surprising in the best possible way.

"Please." Ty's soft word puffs across my skin and spurs me into action.

I touch my lips to Ty's. Something shifts inside of me, like my heart is waking up. Maybe waking up for the first time. I can't remember ever having such a huge reaction to something as simple as the beginning of a kiss.

Our lips brush, then linger. Ty is soft and warm and sweet. I link our fingers together and deepen the kiss, tasting and teasing, my body humming for more. Sliding a hand into my hair and angling his head, he takes control. The slight bite of pain when he fists his hand stokes the flames of want and need. Slipping my tongue into Ty's mouth causes us both to groan. The licks and strokes of tentative exploration grow bolder.

Fighting to control the flame, I force myself to gentle the kiss, to remember that we're in broad daylight, in public, and that climbing onto the table with Ty to take things further isn't a smart idea. For that, I want privacy and zero distractions.

Ty releases the hold he has on my hair and drags his lips away with a sigh. Eyes closed, he keeps his head bent close to mine, like he needs a minute for his system to settle. I can relate because I do too. Too soon, he leans back. "That was nice."

More shaken than I'd expected, I draw in a breath. *Hurricane Ty,* as Slater had said. I'm not ready for our day to end. "Can I take you to dinner?"

"How about I take *you* to dinner?" Ty traces a circle over my palm with his thumb and unleashes a fresh wave of desire.

"We can wrestle for the check later." Joking, of course. I have no intention of letting Ty pay. But the idea of wrestling leads to thoughts of the two of us tangled together in a much more sensuous way.

As physically attracted as I am to Ty, the person beneath the handsome features and soulful eyes is just as intriguing and interesting and I want to know everything about him.

Sultry sounds play from the speakers. We sit tucked away at a tiny table under a neon sign in a dimly lit West Hollywood bar frequented by musicians. It's well past midnight and we've been here for hours, since we left the steakhouse. One drink turned into two, then three. We've traded stories and kisses. At Ty's prompting, I've shared a list of the songs I've written for other artists, and another of the bands I've been in. His promise to put together a playlist makes me smile.

Glass in hand, Ty gestures toward the empty stage at the back of the room. The movement sloshes the liquid close to the rim. "I can picture you on a stage, a guitar strapped across your chest, rocking out. I'm definitely looking up videos of you and your old bands when I get back to the hotel tonight."

"If you want a live version, I'm filling in for a friend at a show tomorrow night." Attempting to keep my voice casual, I trail my fingers over Ty's back. The soft material of his shirt moves as he leans into the touch. My hand meets the belt loop on the side of his jeans. I hook my finger through it and draw him more securely against my chest. "If you want to come."

Ty's hand traces a path up and down my side. His pupils are wide, leaving a thin ring of brown. Licking his lips, he drops his gaze to my mouth. Lingering for a long moment before returning it to my eyes. "Yeah? I'd get to see you in action?"

That questing hand journeys higher and a fingertip brushes over my nipple. Goosebumps dot my skin. I swallow the rest of my drink and set the glass on the table with a clink. My last sentence to Ty came out more like a question, filled with all the hope swirling in my system. Hopefully, the next words will carry more confidence. "You can bring Slater and Noah. I'll put your names on the list."

"I wouldn't miss it." Ty slides his hand up to frame my cheek. The statement is an exhilarating promise of continued time together.

My stumbling nerves over issuing the invitation settle. "Can I kiss you again?"

A smile worthy of a supervillain spreads across Ty's face.

He takes a sip of amber liquid. Wet, tempting lips glisten under the lights. Watching me, he traces his tongue over his lips. "What do you think?"

Unable to hold back, I lean in and lick the same path, tasting alcohol and Ty, heady and rich. He winds his arm around my neck and pulls me in close. The kiss deepens, dragging us into a tidal wave of desire.

The fingers tugging in my hair send frissons of pleasure straight to my cock. I push out of my seat, shifting until I stand between Ty's thighs, and give into need, alternating between grabbing fistfuls of that soft shirt and sliding my fingers along exposed stretches of skin. The kiss changes tempo from soft and slow to hard and fast. On a moan, Ty opens for me, letting me take control.

I have another flash of how we'd be together, in a darkened room, with Ty open and giving under my hands. Letting my thoughts wander too far in that direction isn't smart, not with the way our bodies are brushing together, not with how very much I want the man in my arms, and not with how close I already am to the edge.

Swamped in sensations, I slow the pace to savor once more. Ty's nearness is far more intoxicating than any drink we've consumed. After only half a day, the man has become a craving.

A loud group enters the bar, laughing and celebrating, shattering the sexy private world that included only Ty and me. I pull back and smooth Ty's shirt. "It's pretty late. I should get you back to the hotel. We both need some sleep so you're ready for a full day of comic collecting and I can be functional and alert when manning the foundation's booth in the morning."

He takes a final sip of his drink. "Will you be dressed in a costume again?"

"Not tomorrow. I'll just be me, a non-costumed volunteer, handing out pamphlets and telling people about what we do. As for which superheroes will be there, well, I'll let that be a surprise. Maybe you'll come and find me."

Ty stands and tugs me close once again. "Count on it."

Smiling, I fall into another of his addicting kisses.

I want to count on it—badly. But I've been burned before. Just because someone says one thing doesn't mean they won't end up doing another.

Teasing his lips over mine, Ty slowly raises his head. "I already can't wait for tomorrow."

Hope, sometimes so foreign, settles deep in my bones. Far from being a one hit wonder, the magical day we've spent together is just the beginning.

CHAPTER THREE
TY

The clatter of cutlery on plates and murmur of conversations fills the hotel's dining room. Scents of sausage, waffles, and coffee waft from the breakfast buffet. I shovel in my final forkful of eggs and toast and eye my empty cup of coffee. A night of staying up late listening to all the songs I found by Craig and the various bands he'd been in and played with, and then listening to the ones for other artists where he's credited as the songwriter, followed by a few hours of fitful sleep led to a slow-moving morning. Now at ten AM, I'm already close to two hours behind schedule.

After returning to my room, I text Slater and Noah, and make plans to meet them in the lobby. The buzzed, floaty feeling that's nagged me since I rolled out of bed still lingers. Maybe it's due to the alcohol I consumed last night. Maybe it's the lack of sleep. Maybe it's Craig's kisses. Heat rolls through me as I replay each kiss in my mind.

The songs I downloaded last night from his original band, Falling Midnight, are my playlist while I shower, brush my teeth, and dress. I didn't pack anything except casual clothes, but the black T-shirt and gray shorts are fairly new, and hopefully will look good on me.

I make my way to the lobby. No sign of Slater and Noah, so I settle into a plush chair by a wide window. Hopefully, the sunlight streaming in will clear the cobwebs from my mind.

"Hey, bud." Slater claims the seat across from me, clutching a to-go cup of coffee from the shop at the other end of the lobby. "You look happy. How did it go with Craig?"

"Pretty amazing. Where's Noah?"

"Getting a refill on his tea. Now, back to Craig..." Wagging his brows, he gestures for more info. "Go on."

"We had coffee, then dinner, then went to a bar with really interesting architecture. I drew him a sketch. We did a little drinking, a little kissing..." Ears growing hot, I drain the remainder of my brew. "He's a musician, and he invited me, the three of us actually, to watch him perform tonight at a private concert in a club. He's filling in as a favor to a friend. Would you want to go?"

After taking a sip of his coffee, he nods. "Tonight sounds great. We're in. I'll tell Noah."

"Is it stupid for me to go? For me to want to spend time with him?" Worry and uncertainty rise, weaving a twisted vine up my spine. I push my hand through my hair. "I mean, we're only here for the weekend."

Head tilted, Slater regards me for a long moment, like a wise sage in a superhero T-shirt. "For as long as I've known you, you've been busting your ass working two jobs. You're on vacation. You deserve to have fun, especially with someone who makes you happy."

"I've never had a fling before." Admitting that isn't hard, not to Slater. The hulking hockey player might be a tough guy on the ice, but he's a gentle giant and a supportive friend.

His blue eyes are as kind as his smile. "Sometimes, it's

good to just take the leap. Don't worry so much or overthink. Do what makes you happy. Yes or no, if you don't see him, will you regret it?"

Tapping my fingers on my thigh, I contemplate the advice. I've taken the leap in regard to work, in trying to take my art career to the next level. I know firsthand how regrets can fester over missed opportunities. "You're right. And I would regret it if I missed out on time with him. I really like him."

"Then, you have your answer."

Noah arrives holding two to-go cups. He hands one to me. "That one has coffee. I saw you when I was in line. You look like you need it. Ready to scour the halls for treasure?"

I gratefully accept the cup and sip the strong brew. "You're the best, Noah. I hope Slater appreciates you."

"I appreciate him, and he knows it." Slater pulls Noah against him for a fast kiss. "Let's get going."

The convention center is a fifteen-minute walk from the hotel. I don't mind walking instead of grabbing a ride. The bit of exercise gets my blood flowing and helps clear my head.

The crowds are bigger than yesterday. I hold tight to my list, caught between the desire to search for what I need and to see Craig. If he's working, I shouldn't distract him. So, finding comic books it is. We stop by the closest table. Slater and I reach for the same issue, laugh, and I gesture for him to pick it up. "How'd you make out yesterday afternoon?"

"I found a few things, but we cut out early to get dinner and relax by the hotel pool." With the heated way Slater's looking at Noah, I have zero doubt their time alone included more activities than simply relaxing poolside. Even now, my friends can barely keep their hands off each other.

We follow a snake-like path, working our way down one side of the rows and up the next, winding through the vendors, stopping at each one. I'm not having any luck, but Slater scores a few things he's wanted for a while.

The pull to see Craig grows too strong to ignore. I throw away my empty coffee, pop in a mint one of the vendors was giving away, and glance at the opposite side of the hall, where his booth is stationed. Maybe a quick visit won't interrupt him too much. Jerking my thumb in that direction, I address the guys. "I think I'll make my way over that way. I'll catch up with you later."

After exchanging a knowing look with his boyfriend, Noah pats me on the back. "Have fun."

"Tell Craig we said hi," Slater adds with a smile.

Nerves tightening my stomach, I walk through the sea of people. Anticipation increases with every step. I swipe a speck of lint off my shirt, then smooth a hand through my hair. Rounding the final corner, I slow my pace.

Craig's booth is busy. He stands in front of the table at one end, talking to a small group of attendees while four volunteers costumed as various Avengers characters chat with another group and pose for photos with little kids.

Waiting for a lull in traffic, I peruse the neighboring tables for comic books while I watch Craig. As great as the man looked dressed as a superhero, Craig out of costume can only be described as dangerously handsome. Dark, wavy hair streaked with lighter brown and blond frames a chiseled face. He has tanned skin, a sexy smile, a strong body, and eyes that seem like they can see into my soul. Jeans encase his long legs and a white T-shirt with the foundation's logo stretches across his chest, hinting at the muscles beneath the fabric.

Finally, the group holding Craig's attention breaks away and he returns to the area behind the table. I set the comic book down and head toward him, craving another kiss, another touch, another moment.

Craig turns in my direction. The musician's features lighten with what I hope are welcome and happiness. He beckons for me to join him on his side of the table. "You came. It's good to see you."

"Hi." I can't stop the smile beaming across my face. We're standing close to the spot where I landed in his arms yesterday. "No bodies have catapulted themselves into your space today?"

"Not yet. But there's still several hours to go." Grinning, Craig runs his hand down my arm, a brushing of fingers that's both casual and intimate. "How'd you sleep?"

My body sways toward him as if drawn by a magnetic force. Can I kiss him? Should I? What is Craig expecting? Uncertainty swelling, I gaze into those mesmerizing brown eyes. "I lay awake, thinking about you for a long while. I also listened to the bands you've played in and the songs you wrote for other artists. Caffeine and sugar are the only reasons I'm coherent right now."

"Same here." Craig jerks his head toward the large to-go coffee cup near the end of the table. "Drained that pretty fast, and I feel like my insides are vibrating. Still, totally worth it. Sleep is overrated. Thinking about you, thinking about last night, was a much better way to spend those hours." His voice roughens and his gaze turns heated and hungry. "Ty…"

"Yes?" The word rushes out, just as it did yesterday, filled with an eagerness I can't hide.

Craig's focus slips to somewhere behind me. "Be right back."

I turn to spy what's captured his attention and feel him step away. The crowd is too congested to yield an easy answer. I swing back to find Craig sliding a box sticking out from the table beneath it once more. An attendee from the other side had kicked it out of place. This booth doesn't need more incidents with tripping hazards.

Stepping toward me once again, he smiles at two people approaching the table wearing shirts with the foundation's logo, and lifts his hand in a wave. "My replacements just arrived, which means I'm officially done for the weekend."

If Craig doesn't have to hang around the convention center, will he want to be on his way? Struggling to maintain my smile, I shove my hands into my pockets and mentally kick myself for getting a later start than I'd planned. I'd hoped for more than ten seconds with him. "Oh. Okay."

While Craig greets the newcomers, I edge to the other side of the table, thoughts spinning for some way to prolong our connection. A small group of people who had posed for photos with the volunteers in the superhero costumes have now claimed the newly arrived volunteers' attention. I move over a few more steps until I'm standing in the five feet of space separating the foundation's table and that of another vendor.

"Mind if I tag along with you?" Craig joins me, his fingers plucking at the edge of the leather strap encircling his wrist. He did the same action a few times yesterday, once during dinner and twice during our time at the bar. I don't know him well enough to judge it as a nervous habit, but the hint of vulnerability in his gaze adds to my suspicions. What could a superhero rockstar possibly be nervous about? Does he really think I would turn him away?

"I'd love it." The thought of getting to spend more time with Craig, and the sexy musician wanting to spend time with me, brightens me like sunlight after a storm. I pull my list from my pocket and hold up the creased paper. "Hopefully, we can track down as many of these issues as possible. I didn't find any yesterday, and haven't had luck yet today."

"I'll help you look. I've gotten to know a few of the vendors from doing the convention for the past few years." Craig scans the list and then looks at a map of the vendor floor plan. He taps one of the squares. "I know a guy who probably has all of these."

"All of them?" I gape at him, and the list falls through my grip, fluttering to the floor. I scramble to snatch it up. "You're kidding. That would be like the best thing ever."

"Then I really hope I'm not raising your hopes for nothing." A gentle smile curving his lips, he traces a path down my arm once more. When our fingers brush together, he lingers over the caress, as if tempted to link our hands together. Too soon, the touch falls away. "Let's find out."

We weave through the crowded aisles, Craig calling out greetings and waving to a few vendors along the way. He ducks his head close to my ear and murmurs, "We'll come back to those tables if the first one doesn't have everything. They won't rip you off."

"I really appreciate this." If any of these vendors have good stuff, I'll text Slater so he won't miss out.

Finally, we reach the vendor Craig first pointed out, tucked into a corner. Hundreds of comic books stacked in neat order dominate the shelves, accompanied by vintage figurines in protective packaging. Craig introduces us and I hand over my list.

Resisting the urge to drum my fingers along the table's edge, I lean into Craig's side and watch the vendor sort through stacks that are kept away from any attendee's reach. The warmth of Craig's palm grazes my back, but the fleeting touch fades far too quickly.

One by one, the vendor places the coveted issues in front of me. The small pile grows, along with the excitement swirling through my system. Scoring so many issues at once seems unbelievable, yet it's happened—thanks to Craig.

I take my phone from my pocket. "I need to text Slater. Let him know this guy has good stuff."

"Here, I'll point out the other ones we can visit, so he'll know they're all right." He unfolds the map and runs a finger along the page, pausing at three spots spread across the hall. I type the corresponding table numbers into the message. Text sent, I slip the phone into my pocket.

"I have all but three." The vendor sets my list on top of the books. He gives me a fair price, and I'm within the amount I've budgeted for books this weekend, which means I don't have to put anything back.

After I pay, I thank the guy, and with the bag holding my new treasures in hand, I turn away from the table and bump my shoulder into Craig's. "After how yesterday and this morning went, I was beginning to think I wouldn't find anything. You really are like my superhero."

He waves away the praise. The tips of his ears grow red as he falls in step beside me. "I'm happy you found almost everything you wanted."

We visit the rest of the vendors Craig knows, and I swing between the exhilaration of being with him and the wistfulness of sharing the experience with someone special, someone I might never get to share it, or anything, with again, once the weekend ends.

At the last vendor, we find the final issue I need.

Before I can pull out my wallet, Craig hands a credit card to the woman behind the table. "We'll take it."

I grab his arm, locking my fingers around his biceps. The vintage comic isn't the most expensive of the ones I've bought, but I wouldn't call it cheap either. "I can't let you do that. It's too much."

"I want to." Something sweet and earnest flashes through his features. "Consider it a souvenir from me to you for this weekend."

Every time I see that issue, I know I'll think of Craig, but saying that out loud seems too sappy. "Thank you. Now I owe you a souvenir, too."

"You drew that picture of me." Craig switches his attention to the woman, accepts both the credit card and the bag holding the comic book, then hands the bag to me. He pockets his wallet, calls a thanks to the vendors, and then guides me away from the table. "What else is on your agenda?"

After glancing around to make sure we aren't blocking a path, I twist toward Craig and press a quick kiss to his mouth. The man smells like cinnamon and a hint of something darker. "That."

"That?" A smile plays across his lips. He shifts his body to protect me from the three children running past, brandishing light sabers. Their voices rise and fall as they fly by. "I liked that a lot. In fact, I think I need to experience it again."

Happiness and attraction bolt through my body, lighting up every cell. I link our hands together. "Then let's go."

I draw Craig through the crowded hall and out into the sunshine. Heat covers us like a blanket. We walk until we reach a semi-secluded area shaded by the building's shadow. I set my bags against the wall, then shift until I stand torso to torso with him.

Drawing in a breath, I cup my free hand around the back of his neck. Warm skin and silky hair meet my palm. For a moment, we watch each other. Then, Craig's hands grasp my back and urge me forward, into the circle of his embrace. Our lips meet, and I pour everything I have into the kiss.

Longing. Need. Desire. Want.

Angling my head, I take the kiss deeper. Craig battles me for control, tongue twining with mine as his fingers draw small circles on my lower back. The touches weaken my knees. Moaning, I press our torsos together. Firm muscle lines up against my chest and his semi-hard cock presses into my hip. I can't help a subtle thrust, wanting him to feel my swelling dick, and longing to shed the layers of material separating our bodies. Kissing Craig, holding him, touching him feels so good, far better than holding the most coveted comic book.

Strong fingers press into my body, drawing me even tighter against him, and our tongues duel and thrust, a dance of wet heat. The heady rush of desire makes me lightheaded. I lose myself in the free-fall sensation. Clutching the material at Craig's back provides me with an anchor.

Gradually, the kisses lighten. Craig raises his head and strokes his hand through my hair. I could gaze into his eyes for ages. Lips swollen, we watch each other, our chests pressing together with the rise and fall of our breaths.

A text alert interrupts our wordless admiration of each other with the sound I've chosen for Slater.

"I'd better check that in case he needs something." Sighing, I lower my arms and wait for Craig to do the same. Already missing the feel of his body, I step back, fish out my phone, and relay the message across my screen. "Slater said thanks for the heads up on the vendors. And sent a pic..." I burst out laughing at the image.

"What did he send?"

I angle the phone to show him, knowing I'll have to explain the *I found you* caption posted over a comic book about the Greek gods.

Craig's brows draw together. "I don't get it."

"I'm on the cover. Well, not me, obviously, but my namesake. Typhoeus is my real name."

"That's unique. I've never heard that name before."

I slip the phone into my pocket, scoop my hair out of my eyes, and prepare for seemingly the millionth time, to tell my own origin story. "My dad was really into Greek mythology. Typhon, or Typhoeus, is a monster with one hundred dragon heads. He's known as the father of all monsters. Another name for him is the Storm Giant. I was born during a hurricane, so as the story goes, my father thought the name would be fitting."

"It *is* a cool name. And now, Slater calling you Hurricane Ty makes more sense."

"It's also why I have a soft spot for the villains in anything, including the comic book universes. Typhoeus wasn't one of the good guys. He was a grisly, mighty, deadly monster." Suddenly cold, I cross my arms over my chest. Countless times over the course of my childhood, I'd been teased about my name. And just as many times, I wondered if my parents had chosen the name of a monster because I interrupted and altered their life plans, much like a severely damaging storm can wreak havoc and cause drastic, lasting changes. They sure as hell made me feel that way.

Craig's forehead wrinkles and lines of concern crease around his eyes. He cups his hand over my shoulder. "You look sad. What's wrong?"

Forcing a smile, I lift a shoulder in a half-shrug. "Nothing. Just old thoughts. There were a lot of times I hated my name while I was growing up."

Sympathy softens his features. He closes the distance between us and cups my face in his hands. "I think you're a good guy, Typhoeus. And absolutely nothing like a monster."

Emotion wells at the serious tone and softly spoken

words. The threat of tears shocks me. Obviously, old wounds haven't fully closed. But losing control here, now, won't do. Biting the inside of my cheek helps me gain command of my body. I drop my gaze from Craig's eyes to his lips, then return to getting lost in that deep brown. Forgetting the past is easy with this man in my presence. "I'm glad you think so. I wouldn't want to scare you off."

"There's no chance of that happening." His smiling lips hover close to my mouth. "You're definitely made of hero material."

Not a villain.

Not a monster.

A hero.

The surge of emotions swirls again, lightning fast. I wrap my arms around Craig's strong torso. Holding tight, I bury my face in the space where his neck and shoulder meet and breathe in deep lungfuls of that light cinnamon scent.

Hands caress my back in soothing swirls. The press of a kiss to my hair threatens to unravel me even more. I don't want him thinking I'm a mess. In his arms, I find comfort and feel a safety that surprises me, considering I've only known him a day. Feeling more in control, I raise my head.

Craig doesn't tease, or look at me with anything other than kindness. "You okay?"

I nod. "Sorry."

"Never apologize for that. I liked holding you." And then he kisses me. Soft and sweet, dragging me under to a place where need runs wild and desire roams free. A place where I could happily spend hours, days, years, centuries.

After a while, he raises his head and trails his fingers along my cheek. "How about we find some lunch?"

"Sure." My voice is raspy, and I pause to clear my throat. "My treat, as a thanks for everything today."

Those fingers continue down my neck, then my torso, then over my side until they link with my hand. With a wink, Craig smiles. "We'll see."

I glance at our joined hands. Twenty-four hours ago, I hadn't even met Craig, and now here we are, holding hands, flirting, smiling, kissing, and connecting. A sense of belonging that thrills me.

I pick up my bags and let Craig lead the way, falling in step beside him.

Maybe I don't have anything in common with a mythological monster, but the way my feelings for Craig are forming faster and faster like a hurricane gathering strength is downright scary.

CHAPTER FOUR
CRAIG

The crowd's energy feeds me. Pouring myself into playing, I move around my side of the stage, the lights catching the guitar strapped to my chest. My pre-show nerves are long gone, having worn off before the end of the first song. We're well into our set, and with every note played, I keep searching the crowd for Ty.

Every minute I spend with him leaves me craving more. Lunch together stretched into a full afternoon, then dinner together. If I hadn't had to head to the venue for sound check, we'd probably still be wrapped up in each other.

Holding a guitar, my first love, is an acceptable substitute, but I can't deny how much I enjoy holding Ty.

On the mic at center stage, The Fury's frontman, Luke, sings about love and loss. His powerful voice tears into every corner of the room and every heart.

I move forward for my guitar solo, shredding the fretboard. When I received the call from Luke, asking me to fill in for their guitarist who'd broken his arm, I hadn't anticipated anything other than a night of playing music with one of the first friends I made after moving to LA, but knowing that Ty is somewhere out there increases the pressure for an amazing performance. Losing myself in the music, I let it flood over me.

Light moves over the crowd, and three familiar faces come into view. Just off center stage, Ty stands with Slater and Noah. I catch Ty's gaze and electricity surges through my body. My heart beating faster, I move to the music, rolling my hips a tad more suggestively than my usual style, but I've never had such a captivating audience of one before, either.

Ty's gaze dips to the zipper on my jeans. His tongue peeks out to wet his lips and his focus holds on the sway and thrust. Groaning, I harden. That tongue and those lips wrapped around my cock were the focus of my fantasy as I lay awake, unable to sleep last night. That, and then doing the same to Ty, slowly unraveling him with kisses and caresses until he's breathless and sated and whispering my name.

When Ty's focus journeys back to my face, the naked desire in his eyes tempts me to jump off the stage, grab his hand, and drag him off to someplace where we can play and explore and discover each other's secrets.

Movement to my left jars me from the mini-fantasy. Luke sways closer. I end my solo, diving back into the rest of the hard driving song, and spin toward the singer. The way Luke smirks, I have zero doubt my friend caught me staring at Ty. Grinning, I shrug and go back-to-back with my buddy, playing the melody to accompany Luke's voice belting out the lyrics.

I can't help glancing at Ty again. The light beams over the audience once more, casting a pattern of soft white, then blue, then yellow, painting the people in rapidly changing hues. Wearing a smile, Ty nods along to the beat. He seems to be fully enjoying the show.

Several members of the audience, encouraged by Luke to

sing along, join in with the final chorus. Ty is right there in the mix, singing as he bumps into Noah, then cheers at the song's end.

I strain my hearing, attempting to catch that one voice out of over a hundred. It doesn't work, but I still feel Ty's support, still see those brown eyes shining up at me, that brilliant smile, and those strong hands clapping together.

Ty is surprising in the best possible way. A breath of fresh air. Warm and inviting, friendly and sweet. Sexy and talented. And a damn good kisser. In all the hours we've spent together over the past day and a half, every minute is like unwrapping a new layer of an incredible present.

For the rest of the show, my focus keeps drifting to that spot in the audience, and almost every time, my gaze collides with Ty's. As much as I love playing music, impatience laces through my body, frustrated with anything keeping me from holding Ty, kissing him, talking to him, and exploring our connection. The knowledge that he is flying back home on Monday morning hangs over me like a ticking clock.

After the final song, Luke addresses the crowd. "We love you all. Thank you for being here. Put your hands together for Brendan Gallagher on drums, Landry Marx on bass, and filling in for our boy Zander, Craig Simms on guitar."

I take a bow and wave. Applause and cheers swell and drown out Luke's final message of thanks.

Backstage, I stow my guitar in its case, my movements quickened by my eagerness to get back out on the floor and find Ty. Behind me, the band's members joke and chat. Their friendship reminds me of the bond I share with my original bandmates. "Guys, it's always great playing with you."

Luke pulls me in for a hug. "Thanks for filling in. I owe you one. Want to join us back at my place, or are you heading out?"

"I have someone waiting for me in the bar, but thanks."

A knowing smile graces Luke's lips. "The blond guy you were looking at the whole show? New boyfriend?"

I exchange hugs with Brendan and Landry. "We, ah, just met yesterday."

Luke's smile widens. "So, brand new then. As soon as I saw you today at sound check, I knew something was up. You look happy. It's been a while since I've seen you that way."

"I am happy. Hey, tell Zander I hope he heals quickly."

"Will do. We have a three-week, mini-tour along the coast starting in a few weeks. We're hoping he'll be ready to play by then, but if he's not, are you free to fill in?"

"For you guys? Of course. Text me with details."

"I will. Thanks, man." Luke claps his hand on my shoulder and squeezes. "Appreciate it."

"Night, guys." With a wave, I leave the room.

Luke's voice calls out, "Have fun with your new man. Happy looks good on you, buddy."

Happy.

The word sticks in my mind as I make my way through the crowd of people dancing and drinking. I spot Slater's red hair right away. He, Ty, and Noah stand at the far end of the bar, engrossed in a conversation. Slater glances up, sees me, then nudges Ty.

Ty turns, our gazes collide, and he rushes toward me. I move fast as a flash in his direction, meeting him halfway. Amid a sea of dancers, his face lights with a smile that steals my breath. "You were amazing."

"Thanks." The energy from the show still flows through my veins. The desire to pull him someplace dark and private and use that adrenaline to bring him passion and pleasure is stronger than I anticipated. I reach for Ty, the reflex almost automatic, and he slips into my arms like he belongs there.

Long fingers stroke up my chest, over my neck, and into my hair. Then Ty pulls me forward, directing me down to meet his waiting lips. Instead of the brief brushing I expect, he captures my lips, slanting his head to take things deeper. The kiss is hot, wet, and tastes of whiskey. A thrill rushes through me, like an unexpected dip and spin of a rollercoaster ride.

Ty's tongue strokes the seam of my lips, demanding entry. Groaning, I open, clutching the artist's back. That talented tongue... Those firm lips... My body yearns for the promises Ty is making with his mouth.

Hard, aching, and breathless, I fight for control of the kiss. When Ty allows it, melting against me, I give back as good as I receive, with strokes of my tongue, a nip of my lips, and sliding our torsos together, showing Ty how desperately I want him.

And then I fight even harder to remind myself where we are and how we aren't alone. Gentling my hold, I ease the kiss from sexy to sweet and then made myself lift my head. Ty pulls back, eyes glittering with desire, and an answering call echoes in my blood.

I suck in a breath as scents and sounds of the room slowly come back into focus. Willing my system to level out, I wrap an arm around his waist. His presence, a solid warmth against my side, feels too good and keeps my pulse tingling. I can't let go, can't lose that amazing connection. Curling my finger through the belt loop on the side of Ty's jeans, I walk with him to where his friends wait and then greet Slater and Noah. "Thanks for coming."

A smile curling his lips, Slater glances from me to Ty and back again, then shakes my hand. "Great show, man."

"Can we buy you a drink?" Noah's tone is casual and friendly, but the protective way he and Slater both look at Ty makes it clear they intend to ensure their friend is in good hands.

"Sure." I understand. Hell, I'd do the same thing for any of my buddies. From everything Ty has told me about them, his friends are good guys. There is something about Ty, not quite an innocence, but something fresh and young and effervescent. Of course his buddies would want to look out for him. Even after only knowing him two days, I want to protect him at all costs.

Drinks in hand, we move to a high top table.

Ty sits beside me. His hand casually resting on my thigh is a welcome and comforting weight. "When you said you were filling in for a friend, I didn't know you meant The Fury. They're a huge band."

Multiple platinum records level huge, and now they've added the responsibility of creating and running a music label too, but they're still the guys I know and love. "Luke and I have been friends for years. We met when my old band opened for them on tour."

Smile soft, Ty moves his hand from my thigh to my biceps. His fingertips cover the narwhal's tail. "Is that when you got the tattoo?"

I take a long pull from my bottle of beer and rock the barstool onto its back legs. I've come a long way from the person I'd been back then, when I'd felt immense pressure to live up to the rock star persona. "Yep. Last night of the tour."

A bit of nerves hover on the edges of my concentration. Making a good impression on Ty's friends is important. Letting them sit in the Batmobile may be a point in my favor, but it's not enough. Sipping my beer, I stroke small patterns on Ty's shoulder as we chat with Slater and Noah about their trip, bands they like, my work with the foundation, their off-season training, and the comic book series. Music pulses around us, filling in the spaces as the conversation ebbs and flows.

When the guys finish their drinks, Slater stands and shakes my hand. "We're heading out. Thanks for inviting us tonight."

"See you later." Noah waves at me and then bends to hug Ty. I catch the whispered, "I like him," intended for Ty's ears.

Relief flows as fast as the frenetic beat pounding from the speakers. After the couple walks away, I lean into Ty, lengthening the caresses along his shoulder. "I like them."

"And they liked you." Gaze sparking fire, Ty cups my cheek and slowly strokes his thumb along my stubbled jaw. "I do too."

The words and touch are like a match to kindling. Banked desire flares bright. I slide into Ty's kiss and the flames stoke higher. "Another drink?"

Ty shakes his head. He nips my lower lip and walks his fingers over my chest. "Actually, would you mind if we got out of here?"

Those fingers roam lower, teasing over my stomach, and come to a rest at the top of my jeans. Ty raises a single brow.

Hot and hard, I suck in a breath and capture his hand to hold it in place. "Do you want to go to my place?"

"Yes."

We're kissing before we get through the front door. Distracted by Ty's lips and tongue, I wrestle with my keys, and then my guitar case. I manage to get the door closed and locked and the case propped against the wall, and then Ty is back in my arms.

Darkness surrounds us, but I don't want to stop for a light. Holding him close, I back the artist through my apartment.

In my bedroom, I draw him onto the bed, the mattress creaking under our weight. Muted light from an outside streetlight filters through the edges of the blinds, painting our bodies with a pale wash of gray. I need more, need Ty in full color. Blanketing the long, lanky body, I tap the bedside lamp. A soft, warm glow spills over the bed.

Ty lays under me, lips parted and eyes darkened, and so beautiful. He traces his finger along my jaw. "Kiss me."

Blood buzzing, I shift my weight to my forearms and bring our mouths together. Long moments stretch out as we kiss. Every brush of lips and tease of tongue stokes desire higher. Rock hard, I thrust my hips into Ty's, groaning at the feel of his arousal pressed against mine.

With seeking hands and whispered promises, we move together over the mattress. I can't get enough. Ty is everything warm and giving and wonderful.

Shifting my weight to one arm, I gaze at him. We smile at each other in the dim lighting. "I like you here, in my bed."

"Me too. With you right now, there's nowhere else I want to be."

The soft words touch something deep inside me. They make me yearn. I stroke a possessive path down his torso, from his chest to the bulge in his jeans. With a groan, he rolls his hips into the touch. He tugs my head back into kissing range and his lips and tiny nips of teeth graze along my jaw. Desire flashes fast. I expose my neck for more. My hand tightens over the denim beneath my palm as the scrape of teeth shoots sensations to my cock. "Ty."

"Take your shirt off so I can touch you." Ty ends his order by capturing my lips. He deepens the kiss, thrusting his tongue to mimic the thrusting of our hips.

Breathless, I break the kiss, lean back, and tug my shirt off one-handed. The moment of self-conscious worry if my lover will like what he sees fades at Ty's brows rising in appreciation as his gaze wanders along my body. He reaches out his hands slowly, so slowly, and I hold my breath in anticipation. The touch of his fingertips to my bare chest feels huge. Earth shattering. Random patterns roam over my chest and stomach. Closing my eyes, I moan and revel in the slow strokes. When they move to my nipples and pinch, I arch into the touch. "So good. Harder. Please."

"Like that?" The pressure increases to a burn. Sucking in a breath, I nod. Then fingernails skate across the sensitized areas.

"Oh, fuck." Those zings nearly make me come in my jeans. Biting my lip, I fight for control.

The grazing pauses. "Too much?"

I open my eyes and meet Ty's hesitant gaze. Occasionally, bed partners haven't been comfortable with my wanting pleasure with a little side of pain. Being honest about what I want, what I need, puts me in a vulnerable position, but with Ty, I want to be myself. Nerves quiver, dampening my desire. If Ty rejects me... I take the chance. "It's perfect. So perfect that I—"

The scrape of nails resumes in twin blades of exquisite sensation across each nipple, stealing my breath. Mouth open, I pant, gaze locked on Ty's eyes, my hands curling into the sheets.

All hesitation disappears from Ty's face, replaced by a look of hunger. "You look so sexy with your head thrown back like that."

Lost in pleasure, for a moment, I can't speak, can only feel. My hips move against his, increasing in speed as my heartbeat quickens. The spurt of pre-come is a warning.

Drawing back, I rise onto my knees. Straddling Ty, I push his shirt up his torso. "I need to touch you. This needs to go."

He shifts to sitting and pulls his shirt off. He tosses it on the floor, and then lays before me, a long, lean column of subtle muscles, smooth, pale skin, and low-slung jeans.

My fingers ache to explore. I stretch out beside Ty and draw the man into my arms, gliding my hands over skin that burns hot under my touch. Chest, arms, back, every inch I encounter elicits a response. A gasp, a moan, an intake of breath, a whisper of my name. When I trail my fingers over his stomach, he sucks in a breath and contracts his lower abs as though to help me move closer to the waistband of his jeans. But I'm not ready to rush. I want to savor.

Shifting down the length of Ty's body, I retrace the path of my hands with my lips. Soft kisses to his neck, nuzzling the line of collarbone, and sucking up a small mark in a sensitive spot I discover where his neck and shoulder meet. Gooseflesh dots his skin and he frazzles my concentration with teasing touches of his own. Adorning his chest with kisses, I play with his nipples, gauging his expression to see what he likes best. Kisses and licks and the barest hint of teeth.

I rake my fingers down the center of his torso, following the trail of hair a shade darker than the light dusting of pale blond on his chest. His stomach muscles quiver under my touch and heat radiates from the man. I undo the button and slowly lower the zipper on his jeans. His erection pokes through, covered by light blue boxers. Tracing a single finger over the darker, wet patch on the cotton straining beneath my hand, I bend my head and trail my lips over the soft happy trail.

"Please." Voice desperate, Ty arches his hips.

I ease the jeans and boxers to mid-thigh. Ty's arousal springs free. Shifting further down his body, I lower my head and wrap my hand around his cock. Watching his face, I swipe my tongue along the length from root to tip. Then do it again, slower, teasing my tongue over heated skin as my lips journey higher. When I reach the crown, I lave the area with my tongue, tasting pre-come, and linger on the spot that makes him toss his head back and clutch the sheets. His legs, trapped in denim, move restlessly. His hips flex, and I detour to trace my tongue along the indentation near the hipbones forming the V.

He moans and tangles his hands in my hair. "Please," he says again, "more." And gently pulls me back to his cock.

I swirl my tongue around the head once again. Watching Ty's face, I wrap my hand around the base, then take the head into my mouth and suck. His lips part, panting, and his eyes mist in pleasure. Ty's hips buck and his fingers tighten, pulling my hair.

The bite of pain spikes my desire. I tighten my fist and hollow my cheeks, sucking harder. When the grip on my hair slackens a bit, I pull off his cock, range over his torso, and place my index finger on swollen, parted lips. "Get it wet for me."

Seconds pass while I wait for Ty to process my words. Pupils fully blown, he takes my finger into his mouth. He sucks hard and works his tongue around the digit, and I ache to feel that mouth around my cock. My jeans grow impossibly tight. I pop the button and ease the zipper down, gaining some relief. When his fingers graze my cock, I shift out of reach and withdraw my finger. "If you touch me now, I'll explode."

I slip back into position straddling his legs. Stroking his cock, I close my lips over the head. My other hand plays with Ty's balls before moving farther back to rub circles over his rear entrance, then ease my wet fingertip inside him. His gasps and moans and muttered words are a guide and a turn-on, amping up my desire until it feels like I'm walking a tight rope on an electrical wire.

Groaning, he tugs my head closer, pushing himself deeper, and arches his hips over and over. "So good," *pant*, "so close," *pant*, "Craig," *pant*. The words huff out and he tosses his head into the pillow. Then his grip on my hair tightens and he releases one hand to tap my head in warning. "I'm there."

I clamp both my hands onto his hips and take him deeper. Relaxing my throat, I swallow around the head and hum. The air fills with Ty's steady moans. The mattress moves as his arms fling out and his body jerks. Salty release floods my mouth.

Tightening my hold, I drink him down, and then gently suck on the softening cock, coaxing more tremors and moans from the lanky, sexy man. When Ty's body finally calms and his grip on my hair shifts to caresses, I ease back. He looks shattered, in the best way. Clamping hold over my own desire, I kiss my way up his body.

The lamplight catches his glittering gaze. He traces his fingers along my cheek. "That was… wow. And I didn't even get my jeans all the way off."

"I can take care of that." Shifting to the foot of the bed, I tug Ty's socks, jeans, and boxers off, and then strip out of my clothes. I grab a bottle of lube from the bedside table, hand it to Ty, and resume my place by his side. "Whatever you want."

"I want to start by touching you. Sit up for me." Ty moves behind me and after a moment, the weight of his hands presses into my shoulders and kneads the muscles. The massage continues over my back, alternating between rough and soft touches.

"Oh, that's nice." I lean into the long strokes and sigh when Ty trails kisses over my neck.

"I love your muscles. Love watching them jump and flex under my hands."

At Ty's words, pleasure and pride lace through me. The man's touch is addicting. "I love feeling your hands on me."

Ty slips his arms around my torso, locking us together, back to front. I lay my hands over his, trapping them in place and try my best to absorb every sensation, scent, and feeling of being wrapped in his arms and commit it to memory.

Releasing my hold lets me move my hands to rest on Ty's thighs. The massage continues. His roaming hands trek over my chest and stomach. Clever fingers tweak and roll my nipples. Anticipating his hands where I long to feel them most, I stroke my aching cock. He continues the kisses along my neck, graduating to nips of teeth.

Groaning and rock hard, I press my head into the crook of his neck and shoulder. "Ty, you're killing me. It's so good."

"Sit with your back against the headboard." The low command feathers over my cheek before Ty draws away.

I quickly comply, desire ratcheting as I scramble over the mattress.

Ty kneels in front of me, between my splayed legs. With a smile, he leans in until we're sharing breath. "That's better."

Before I can respond, he takes my mouth in a sultry, sexy kiss. The meeting of lips is so intimate and intense, I could gladly spend hours on this act alone. Our tongues tangle, and soon, the sensation of his fingertips grazing my inner thighs join in, raising my anticipation as those talented fingers edge closer to my weeping cock. It points straight up, curving toward my stomach.

"Touch me." I'm not above begging.

Smile wicked, he pours a small amount of lube and works

my length with both hands. With a tight grip, he pulls one hand then the other from base to head, over and over again. My head tips back and my eyes fall closed. Ty's touch is amazing. Then he switches to a twisting motion at the head of my cock that brings me to the edge of my control.

Holding tight to his shoulders, I buck my hips. "Ty…"

He kisses me again and draws my bottom lip through his teeth. "I'm going to make you feel so good. Just hang on for me for another minute."

After drizzling more lube over his hand, he continues with his just on the right side of rough grip along my throbbing cock. That twist at the head focuses on my most sensitive spot. Then he switches to a dual assault, working one hand up and down the shaft while the other concentrates on the head, exploiting my every curse and sigh, every moan and gasp—twisting, gliding, rubbing—driving me higher and higher. I strain toward him, ready to burst. And then Ty presses his thumb into my slit.

"Just like that." Pleasure spiraling through me, I arch into his touch. "Don't stop."

The scrape of teeth at my neck and the slice of a fingernail across my nipple join the rushing sensations and push me over the edge. I yank him against me, writhing as my release shoots onto our chests. He keeps jacking me, sucking kisses on my neck, absorbing my quakes with a sexy moan about how good I look coming apart under his hands.

Floating through sensations, I become aware of his hand stroking my hair. Caring caresses have never been a part of any hookup I've had. Everything with Ty is unique, and better. My breathing evening out, I rest my head against the headboard and adjust my arms around Ty's shoulders, keeping him close in my embrace. "That was amazing."

He kisses my temple. "It was. You are."

We exchange kiss after kiss. Stickiness on my chest finally forces me from the bed. I pad to the bathroom, clean up, then run a washcloth under warm water and return to the bedroom with it. Ty takes the cloth with a thanks, and wipes himself down.

After tossing the cloth in the clothes hamper, I climb into bed. Ty welcomes me with a smile. I stretch out beside him, slip an arm around his shoulders, and he raises his face for a kiss. Our lips meet and I linger, soft and slow, trying to pour all of my feelings into the kiss. Happiness, gratitude, and a contentedness I want to feel always.

When we part, he traces a finger along the scar on my chin. "How did you get this?"

"During a show. We had another band on stage with us for the finale. Their guitarist swung his guitar without looking and it caught me."

He presses a kiss to the thin line. "That must have hurt."

"So freaking bad. It bled a lot, and I needed a ton of stitches. I'm just grateful it happened at the end of a show." The memory isn't a pleasant one, but I smile, touched, because Ty kisses the scar again. A kiss to make it better.

He shivers and cuddles closer.

"Cold?" Without waiting for an answer, I tug the blanket from the foot of the bed over the sheet. "I like to keep the air conditioning turned low when I'm sleeping. Nothing worse than trying to sleep in a too hot room. But I don't want you to be cold."

He smiles as I tuck the blanket around him. "I'm fine with the blanket. It's even better with your arm around me."

I resume my original position and wrap an arm around him again. "How's that?"

"Perfect." Stifling a yawn, he tucks his head into the

crook of my neck and snuggles in. His body slowly sinks as he falls asleep.

I turn off the light. It's late, but sleep isn't coming. Tracing my hand along Ty's spine, I let myself wonder what things could be like if he lived in LA. How things would be if we had more than one weekend together.

Maybe we can keep seeing each other long-distance and fly out to visit each other every few months.

But would Ty even want to keep in touch when he gets back to Buffalo? And if he does, would the demands of real life step in and have us drift apart? The connection with this man is deeper than anything I've experienced with anyone. The idea of not having it leaves a hollowness in my gut.

Nothing lasts forever. I've always done my best to enjoy what I have while I have it. But Ty is too perfect, too special, too amazing to only be in my life for a mere two days. Fate wouldn't be that cruel, would it?

Ty is more than a one weekend type of guy. He is a forever type of guy. And I'm not anywhere near ready to say goodbye.

CHAPTER FIVE
TY

I wake to sunlight streaming through the bedroom window and enchanting notes from an acoustic guitar drifting from the hall. Not wanting to miss Craig playing, I toss the covers aside, stand, stretch, and then pad into the bathroom.

A fresh set of clothes, towels, and a new toothbrush are in a neat pile on the sink. Smiling at Craig's thoughtfulness, I quickly clean up. The gray athletic pants have a drawstring waist which helps convert them close to my size. They still bag a little, but rolling the waistband a few inches helps. The light blue T-shirt is the softest cotton I've ever felt. It's a size too big, but I don't care. Wearing Craig's clothes, especially after the night we shared, makes me feel extra close to the man.

The music continues to play. I pause at the entry to the living room. Craig sits in a chair by the window, dressed only in jeans, strumming the guitar. What a picture he makes, with the light playing across his skin. My fingers itch for my sketchbook.

A floorboard creaks when I shift. Craig's attention snaps in my direction. He smiles and the music fades. "Morning."

"Hi." I wander farther into the room, taking in the light gray walls, dark gray throw rugs, a piano, two guitars, and a small black couch. Last night, I was too consumed by Craig to get more than a passing glance at the space.

He sets the guitar in its stand next to an electric guitar and an amp much smaller in size to the ones that had been on the stage during the band's performance. "Hungry?"

"Starving." My heartbeat stutters as he walks toward me, and again when he leans in close and brushes our lips together. I splay my hands across his muscled chest. Heat seeps into my skin and I wish I'd held off on slipping into clothes before wandering the apartment to find Craig. "Have you been awake long?"

"A while." Linking our fingers together, he leads the way to the kitchen. Peering at the microwave clock, he raises his brows. "No wonder I'm hungry. It's been a few hours since I got up. I'm sorry I wasn't there when you woke, but I've learned the hard way that when I wake up with lyrics and melodies in my head, I need to get them down right away or risk losing them forever."

"I lose all track of time when I'm creating things too." The gray and white theme continues in this room. I spy the sketch I'd given Craig hanging on the refrigerator. "You kept it."

He presses a button on the coffeemaker, then takes mugs out of the cabinet. "Of course I did. I'm going to frame it. How about pancakes for breakfast?"

"I'll eat anything." Pleasure surges at the thought of my sketch hanging on one of Craig's walls. Ready to help with the cooking, I lean against the counter, and set the ingredients he passes me in an organized row. "What are you up to today?"

"There's a huge team visit at Children's Hospital this afternoon. Most of our volunteers are taking part." He hands me a carton of eggs and his expression turns thoughtful. "Would you want to come? You could wear a costume. We don't have any villains, but there are a ton of hero choices in the vault at headquarters."

"I'd really like that." Not only do I want to go so I get to see Craig in action and spend more time with the man, but also because the whole idea of the foundation and what they do to spread joy impresses the hell out of me. I want to be a part of it.

Craig pauses with a bag of flour in his hands. Lines of concern crease his face. "Today is the last day of the convention."

I lay my hand on top of his, and press a kiss to his cheek. "I'm fine with missing it. Spending the afternoon with you, hanging out and making sick kids smile is a much better option."

The lines fade away and he beams. "Okay, good. I'm glad."

"So, where's your pancake recipe?"

He taps his temple. "Right here."

I stay close as he whisks together the batter and help by washing a carton of blueberries then add them to the mixture. He puts me in charge of making scrambled eggs while he monitors the pancakes and flips them with precision. Soon, we have a stack ready and full plates.

The pancakes are sweet and the tartness of the blueberry explodes on my tongue. "This is really good."

"I'm glad you like it." Craig smiles at me over the rim of his coffee mug. "And I'm glad you're coming with me later. I can't wait for you to see the kids."

"How did you get started with the charity?"

"One of my old bandmates, the band I was in after Cody and Devon went back to Buffalo, had a son who had leukemia. He loved superheroes, and was pretty sad about being stuck in the hospital. So that Halloween, my buddy threw a little party for him in the hospital room. We all dressed as superheroes. His son dressed up too. Everyone had a blast. And I saw how excited the other kids on his floor were to see us. So a few weeks later, we went back, dressed up again to visit everyone. Then did it again. And again. It turned into a tradition and we formed the foundation soon after."

Sympathy swells as I picture the scene Craig painted with his words. "That's amazing. And your bandmate's son… Did he…"

Craig's smile becomes a full-blown grin. "He is now a healthy, happy ten-year-old."

Breath I hadn't realized I'd been holding rushes out. "That's good."

"Yeah. He was one hell of a fighter. I'm glad he gets to just be a kid now."

After we finish eating, Craig makes fresh cups of coffee and we carry them into the living room. Carefully sipping the rich brew, I tap a couple of piano keys. Tiny clinks of the highest notes ring out. I glance at Craig. "I always wanted to learn how to play."

"I could teach you." The offer rolls off his tongue quickly, and from his serious expression, he means it.

Ignoring the fact that I'm leaving tomorrow, and thinking Craig might be doing so too, I set my coffee on a side table next to the couch and sit at the piano bench.

Craig stands behind me. Strong hands rest on my shoulders. "Put the fingers of your right hand on the center keys."

"All right." Feeling a little silly, I comply. Then smile as Craig's hand covers my fingers.

"Now, you're going to learn the first song I learned to play when I was a kid. It's easy, and it only uses five notes. Just relax your fingers under mine. Let me do the work."

"Deal." I relax my shoulders and rest my head against his torso and watch our joined hands. With subtle pressure, he presses his index finger, then his middle finger. Those two notes echo each other eight times. Then one note from the key under my thumb, followed by a single note for each key under each finger, from my index to my pinkie. We go back down the keys and then up once more, ending with the high note from the pinkie's key.

He lifts his hand and returns it to my shoulder. "Good. Now you try it."

My heartbeat ticks up. I straighten my posture. Even though it's a simple song, I really want to impress Craig. I start off with the two echoing notes, then go up and down the scale, trying to remember the tempo he used. The last note fades, and I hold my breath, nervous for his response.

"You did it!" Squeezing my shoulders, Craig bends and kisses my cheek. "Nice job."

Pride surging, I tilt my head back for another kiss. I catch his smile and then that firm mouth covers mine in a sexy, sort of upside-down kiss. When we separate, I pat the space beside me on the bench. "Will you play something for me?"

"Sure." He climbs over the bench and lays his hand on my thigh to keep me in place. "Stay. I like having you here."

Hands hovering over the keys, he presses his lips together and stares at the wall. Then he smiles and dives into playing. Both hands travel over the keys. The melody is vaguely familiar, then recognition dawns. It's a version of one of The Fury's ballads. Normally played on an acoustic guitar, the song was a huge recent hit for the band. The piano gives it an almost ethereal quality. Then Craig's raspy voice adds the lyrics, and my jaw nearly hits the floor. Hauntingly beautiful, the song which sings of love and longing, pulls at my soul. His talent calls to the artist in me, and a vision of mornings sketching while he plays dances through my head. But I shake the fantasy away as quickly as it came.

Shifting my position, I straddle the bench, facing him. No sheet music is in sight. He's playing the song from memory. Shirtless and sexy, and fully into the music, Craig at the piano is every bit as tempting as Craig on guitar. Once again, I wish I had my sketchbook.

The song reaches its end, and the higher notes that had kept Craig leaning into my torso as he reached for those keys fade into silence. He meets my gaze and the shyness there is so unexpected, I wrap my arms around him, encircling him halfway before my brain catches up with my actions. "You were amazing."

"You liked it?"

"I loved it." I stroke my hand through his thick hair, loving the way the soft strands tease my palm. "So much that I wish I had a video. Your voice is so good. Why weren't you ever a lead singer?"

"I don't like being the center of attention that much."

I pause mid-stroke. "You looked like you loved being in the spotlight during your solo last night."

"Yeah, but all I cared about then was putting on a show for *you*." Finally, his smile forms. "Did you happen to notice how I looked at no one else but you?"

"I did, actually." Pleasure spikes as images from last night fill my thoughts. "And I don't think I was the only one who noticed."

"Luke noticed too. And I'm sure there were more."

"Slater and Noah did too." I lightly tug on the strands in the way I discovered Craig liked last night. "I like having you at the center of my attention."

On a moan, his eyes close and his hands tighten on my chest and thigh. "Likewise."

Our mouths meet and I deepen the kiss. He tastes of maple syrup and coffee, sweet and rich. My hands roam the expanse of tan skin, and I sigh and arch into his questing hands. Lengthening kisses and lingering touches shift the lazy morning into an urgent rush to be as close as possible.

Craig stands, pulling me along with him, and tugs my body until it's snug against his hard form. I shoot my hand out for balance and it lands on the black and white keys, releasing a jumbled tangle of notes.

"Let's take this somewhere more comfortable." He climbs over the piano bench and holds out his hand. Grasping it, I wait to see where he'll lead me. The couch is close by, the throw rug would do, and the bed has the most space.

"Where to?"

"The bedroom." His lips curve in a sexy smile. "What we did last night deserves a repeat performance."

The afternoon sun is high and hot, beaming in a cloudless sky. Being dressed as the Flash tickles me. I hustle with Craig along the crosswalk in front of Children's Hospital's main entrance, my nerves swarming my system. The doors open and we step into the cool relief of air conditioning.

At the foundation, when I'd selected the costume and met the volunteers, I was briefed on the workings of a usual visit, but not knowing exactly how everything will go, and worry over the possibility of failing to make the kids happy, knots my stomach.

The rest of the volunteer group files in behind us. We traveled together from the foundation's headquarters in a caravan of three cars with the foundation's logo. Dressed in colorful costumes, they are a happy, exuberant team and welcomed me with a level of inclusion I, a newcomer known to be here for only one visit, hadn't expected.

We gather by the security desk and wait for the hospital staff person who coordinated the visit.

Craig, dressed in a Superman costume, turns toward me and links our hands together. "I'm really glad you're here."

"Me too. I hope I do a good job." I glance down at my costume. "And I hope there aren't any occurrences of Hurricane Ty. Banging into something in one of the rooms could potentially be really bad."

"You're *Superhero* Ty today." Craig's voice is gentle and his hold on my hand tightens. "And you're nowhere near the walking disaster you labeled yourself when we met."

Glad my costume hides the flush of heat creeping over my neck and face, I shrug. "I was a pretty accident-prone kid, so I earned that nickname back then."

"Other than the display table, have you had anything else happen lately?"

I click through my mental file. "Nothing that big. Nothing that required medical attention for myself or caused damage to someone else. Not in years."

"There you go, then." With a smile, he bumps our shoulders together. "Relax. This visit will be fun. And no matter what happens, I'm here."

Those last two words shroud me in protection and ease my worries. And make me fall harder for the man. I squeeze his hand. "My hero."

The clicking of heels on the tiled floor announce the coordinator's arrival. After we volunteers are approved by hospital security, we begin our rounds from room to room. Sticking close to Craig, I greet the patients and parents, pose for photos, and help hand out activity packets. I love the children's reactions to our costumes. My favorite is the huge, professional body builder painted green like the Hulk.

In every room, Craig speaks to parents and children with an ease I envy. While he chats, I do quick sketches of any character the children request. The smiles I receive are priceless.

Watching Craig throughout the afternoon raises my opinion of him even more. Not every man would give up hours of his weekend to volunteer, and pour himself so wholeheartedly into the role. Craig is someone special, and my chest pinches as our time together hurls faster and faster toward its end.

We wrap up our visit with a group photo of all the volunteers and members of the hospital staff who coordinated the visit.

After the photo is taken, Craig pulls me aside and holds up his phone. "Take a selfie with me?"

"Great idea. I want one on my phone, too." I pull my phone from a side pocket sewn into my suit. "This is the first time I've ever been in a hero costume. I'm always a villain."

"Really? Even back when you were a kid?"

"Even then." Huddling in close, I smile at our image on his screen. We look good together. Better than good, we look perfect.

The passage of time weighs heavy on my mind as we return to the foundation, and as I bid goodbye to the costume and the other volunteers, and again during the drive with Craig to my hotel. Meeting him Friday afternoon, our time together at the coffee shop and the bar, searching for comic books together on Saturday, then lunch, exploring the city, dinner, the concert, sex, sleeping together, waking up this morning to Craig on guitar, making pancakes, the piano lesson, the hospital visit... all of it, every single moment has spun by so fast. Every passing minute is too easily visualized as sand slipping through an hourglass.

We stop at a red light. Craig lays his hand on my thigh. "You're quiet."

I manage a smile. "Just looking at the scenery." And thinking. So much thinking.

"What time is your flight tomorrow morning?" The tentative question pokes into the heart of my musings. His posture tightens, as though he's bracing himself for the answer, and knowing in advance he isn't going to like it.

Maybe I'm not the only one sad about our time together coming to an end. "We have to be at the airport by six."

"Damn, that's early. I wish you were taking a flight later in the day." With a gentle squeeze, Craig turns his attention back to the road. The light changes to green, and he leaves his hand on my thigh as he drives. The weight is comforting and breaks my heart a little more. No way do I want to get on that plane. After a few minutes, I lace our fingers together. His hand feels so good, and so right, in mine.

The hotel comes into view and my stomach fills with dread. I'm not ready to say goodbye. My hand tightens around his. The car rolls slowly through the crowded parking lot.

Unsure of whether he intends to stop by the entrance and drop me off, or find a space, I twist toward him, drinking in his profile. The car turns down one row and then he swings into a space near the middle of the lot. He gently extracts his hand from my grip and turns off the engine.

Playing with the edge of his leather bracelet, he meets my gaze. "Do you have plans with Slater and Noah tonight?"

I shake my head. My friends know I want to be with Craig. We exchanged texts earlier, right before I'd gone to the hospital visit. "Can you stay a while?"

He captures my hand, raises it to his lips, and feathers a kiss along my knuckles. "Until you kick me out."

The thought immediately flashing into my mind makes me laugh, and I give voice to it. "Then I guess you're staying the night."

"You won't see me complaining about that." After another kiss, Craig releases me and we climb out of the car.

Inwardly, I cheer. Staying the night means I have another good twelve hours with him. I intend to make the most of them.

When we reach my room, I flick on the light, kick off my sneakers, and gesture for Craig to make himself comfortable. The room has two double beds and a separate seating area. Everything from the walls to the bedding to the furniture is decorated in shades of cream.

We order room service and eat sandwiches stuffed with grilled vegetables and chicken on herb-encrusted bread, crispy fries seasoned with pepper and sea salt, and drink wine while sprawling out side by side on one of the beds, talking about everything from the serious to the silly. Sharing. Kissing. Touching. Tasting.

Dinner finished, we feed each other bites of the chocolate mousse we ordered for dessert, our hands roaming over each other's bodies and stealing kisses between each taste offered. The rich chocolate melts on my tongue. I raise the last spoonful to Craig's lips. Eyes heavy with desire, he accepts the offering. I quickly set the bowl and spoon on the tray. When I turn back, he is right there, with a chocolate-flavored kiss.

On a moan, I thread my hands into Craig's wavy hair, desperate for the promises of that talented mouth. Strong hands slip over my skin, pushing my shirt out of the way. I maneuver over the mattress, pulling him down with me, until we're laying comfortably across the bed.

In between kisses, we cast our shirts, pants, boxers, and socks into a pile on the other bed. Tangled together, heated skin lined up, cocks touching, legs rubbing, torsos brushing, we fall into kiss upon kiss.

Craig's hands play over my skin, as skilled in the knowledge of my body as he is with a guitar or piano. Driven high into sparking passion, I gasp and moan as my every secret is exposed.

Throbbing for more, I skate my hands down his sides and slip them between our bodies. My hand around his cock, stroking the hard flesh, has him moaning and thrusting into my grasp. I slide the other up his chest to tweak a pebbled nipple. "I want to feel you."

In a swift roll, he shifts us from laying side-by-side to him ranging over me, his chocolate-laced breath feathering over my lips. "How? Where? You can have whatever you want."

The previous two times we've been together, we've traded hand jobs and blow jobs. As satisfying as those experiences were, this time, I want more. "I want you in me."

Desire flares in those brown eyes and Craig pulls me into an enthusiastic kiss. Our tongues tangle and torsos rock together. "I have a condom in my wallet. After what happened last night and this morning, I wanted to be prepared."

My cock surges at the memory of the mutual blow jobs we gave each other after breakfast in his sun-drenched bed and how he edged me with his fingers and tongue. "I like that you're prepared. I didn't expect anything to happen on this trip, so I have nothing with me."

With a quick kiss, Craig rolls off the bed. In the absence of his heat, coolness rushes in. I watch the muscles in his back and legs flex as he bends to retrieve his wallet. He straightens, holding the condom and a small packet of lube. After setting the items on the bedside table, he stretches out beside me, pulling me against his long form. I sigh at the full-length press of heated skin. He dives into kissing me like it's the very reason for his existence. We roll together, switching positions—top, bottom, over, under—driving each other higher with every touch.

"I'll get you ready." Breathless, he wraps his hand around my dick. The callouses on his fingers add a hint of roughness and I thrust into his fist. I don't like or need bits of pain like Craig, but this roughness is just right.

Desperate to return pleasure, I work his cock, too, drinking in every gasp leaving the musician's lips.

He tears into the lube packet and dribbles some onto his fingers. Leaning on one arm, he kisses me as his other hand plays at my rim, teasing before edging a single digit inside.

My breath catches as the sensation grows bigger, deeper. I glance from Craig's face down to where his fingers are disappearing into my body. One finger, then two. Then, a third.

Grasping his shoulders, I lose myself in another kiss. My cock leaks steadily. I need more than those fingers. "Craig, please."

"Whatever you want." He leans back and grabs the condom. Before he puts it on, I take the lube and pour some into my palm. Then take hold of Craig, rubbing the slickness along his shaft and encouraging him to thrust into my tight fist. Groaning, he does just that, then abruptly pulls away. "Too close. Way too close."

After he rolls the condom down his length, he settles between my legs and nudges them farther apart. One hand braced on the bed, he ranges over me, his gaze tracing a path up my body to meet my gaze. "Ready for me?"

My heartbeat hammers and nerve endings quiver in anticipation. "So ready. I want to feel you."

He lines up his cockhead with my hole and my breath catches as he gently presses forward. With a sharp intake of breath, he eases inside, pausing every few seconds. The sensation of him opening me up is so good. His teeth sink into his bottom lip and his features draw tight. "I know it's been…" He sinks deeper, "a while for you… " Another inch, and he finishes his sentence through a clenched jaw, "I don't want to hurt you."

Warmth washes into my chest and I moan as he slides the rest of the way home. He holds himself there, hard and thick, and so deep inside me. Hands resting on either side of my head, he brings our lips together.

We kiss as I grow used to the fullness, until the need for him to move becomes too great. I stroke my thumb along his jawline. "I'm ready. Give me more."

His hips retreat until just the head of his cock remains inside me, then pushes forward all the way in one slow advance. I let my head fall against the pillow as his movements grow bigger, get deeper, shattering me with sensations.

Resting his weight on one arm, Craig holds my gaze and runs his other hand down the center of my chest in a possessive streak. That touch sends me soaring. I want to belong to him, for us to belong to each other. The warm palm travels over my stomach and then wraps around my dick. I arch into the touch, trying to take him deeper. "You feel so damn good."

"You too. So tight around me." Shallow thrusts punctuate each word. Then they pick up speed.

Faster. Harder. Deeper. The pace increases with every beat of my heart.

I dig my heels into his ass, pulling him closer. Pleasure

races through me, my fingers clawing at the bedsheet. My release slams into me, white hot and blinding, and I cry out, spurting over his hand and onto my stomach. As I come down, I feel Craig's cock swell. Wanting to push him over the edge, I scrape my nails over his nipples and sink a love bite into his shoulder.

With a groan, he thrusts forward. Head thrown back, he closes his eyes. His muscles strain and his mouth drops open in soundless release. Muted heat fills the condom.

Completely sated, I stroke my hand down his chest. "I love the way you look when you come."

His eyes open. He falls forward, supported by his hands on either side of my shoulders, then drops onto his forearms. "Yeah? You look pretty amazing that way too."

I slip my hands behind his neck and urge him closer, into a kiss. The endorphins floating through my system have me flying high. I feel good—great, actually—and it's all thanks to Craig.

Hand in hand, we walk to the bathroom and clean up, then slip back into bed, sharing the last of the wine. The hour grows late, and there's still one more story to tell, and one more kiss to savor.

In the early hours of the morning, I fall asleep in Craig's arms, wishing I could hold him forever.

The blaring of the alarm clock crashes through my dreams. I blearily roll toward the sound and stab the button to silence the noise. Green digits glow the time. Five AM.

Craig groans and wraps his arm around me, drawing me back into the heat of his body. "Feels like we just fell asleep."

"I have to get ready." But I don't make a move, snuggled

into the embrace. With each change of a digit on the clock, minutes tick by and tension tightens through me like a strangling snake. Finally, the time clicks to the absolute last minute I can stay in bed. My heart heavy, I press a kiss to Craig's hand and then slip out from under his arm.

The fresh mint of my toothpaste helps wake me up a little and the shower's hot spray chases away the chill of the room's air-conditioning. Bracing my hands on the tiles, I lean into the water rushing down like an intense rain shower. I need a minute to fully chase away the cobwebs of sleep clouding my mind.

A gentle knock on the bathroom door, and then it eases open and Craig steps inside the room, gloriously naked. After a quick swirl of mouthwash, he comes closer. "Mind if I join you? I know we have to hurry, but I…"

"I know." Wanting to share every last minute, I pull back the curtain. Craig slips in behind me, so warm, and wraps his strong arms around my waist, pulling our bodies together. Pressing kisses to my temple, he grabs the small bottle of body wash and pours the clear liquid into his hands.

Luxuriating in the feel of the soapy slide of his hands over my skin, I lean my head onto his shoulder. "This is nice."

"It is. I'm bummed I didn't think to do this with you yesterday morning at my place."

His warm hand slides over my hardening cock, and I push my hips forward into the touch. Why had the guys and I decided to take such an early flight? Can I miss it? But what if I have trouble getting a later one? I have to be back at the office bright and early tomorrow. Those hands move to my hips and with a gentle pressure, urge me to turn so I'm facing Craig.

A sexy smile and half-lidded gaze greet me. I slide my arms around him and rub our torsos together, transferring soap and wishing I had more time to play. Our mouths meet and our stubbled chins and cheeks add pinpricks of sensation to the kiss. Craig's hands resume their strokes along my back and I arch into the mini-massage. Strong fingers cup my ass, pulling me tighter into his body. As they stroke circles over my skin, sparking arousal, I return the favor, skating my hands over as much skin as I can reach.

Keeping his hold on me, Craig turns us so he's standing under the spray. "I'll rinse off, then start some coffee. Let you finish up in here."

After one more kiss, he steps out of the shower. My gaze on him exiting the room with a towel wrapped around his waist, I drop the shampoo bottle.

Time is ticking away too quickly to waste any minutes. I rush through washing my hair, rinse off, towel off, then leave the bathroom, finger-combing my hair.

The scent of coffee fills the room. Craig is dressed and pouring two steaming cups from the small coffee machine on the desk. Hair in a wavy mess around his face, he crosses the room and hands one to me.

I take a careful sip. Fragrant and rich, the liquid is a touch too hot to drink. "Thank you."

With him watching, I tug on clothes and toss items into my suitcase. My hand pauses over the borrowed athletic pants and shirt I wore yesterday. "What about these? I feel weird handing back dirty clothes. Do you want me to—"

"Keep them." Craig's rushed words remind me of the times I've spoken so quickly and earnestly when responding to his questions about spending time together. Maybe he wants to be sure I won't forget him. The tips of his ears redden. "You looked better in them than I ever could."

"Okay. Then, thanks." Knowing I'll wash and then slip them on as soon as I land, and certain they'll take first place among my favorite things to wear, I tuck the clothes into my bag. Finished packing, I leave a tip for housekeeping, then pick up my coffee and join Craig sitting on the bed. Our hands link together, just as they had last night when we lay together talking.

Sipping the strong brew, I keep glancing at the clock. Nerves fill my stomach. I don't know what to say, how to possibly articulate all that the weekend, all that Craig, meant to me.

"How much time do we have left?" His soft question hangs heavy in the air.

I set my cup on the bedside table. "Just a few minutes."

Stretching past me, Craig places his cup beside mine. Then he stands and pulls me up too so we're hip to hip and heart to heart. He raises our joined hands and studies the way they fit together. "This weekend was… incredible."

"I…" I tighten my hold, locking our hands together. My swift intake of breath draws Craig's attention from our hands to my gaze. Every cell in my body resists stepping away from the man in front of me. "I'm glad I met you."

"Me too. You can crash into my display table anytime." Smiling, he caresses my palm with his thumb in slow, steady circles. His eyes are eloquent as he frames the left side of my face with his other hand. "I'll call you."

I'll call you. So often an empty promise or a brush off. But the sincerity in Craig's gaze compels me to believe him.

"I will, too." I mean it. No way do I want to lose touch.

A soft knock on the door breaks the silence.

Even though I've been expecting it, my heart rate spikes. Time is up. I release my hold and force myself to take a step away. "That'll be Slater and Noah."

Craig nods and his hand falls away from my face. Moving

aside to let me pass, he gestures toward the bags stacked in the corner. "I'll help carry your stuff down."

"Thanks." Smoothing my shirt and hair, I walk to the door. My reflection in the mirror on the wall makes me pause. Dark circles under sad eyes. I flip the lock and tug the door open.

Slater and Noah stand in the hall, travel bags in hand. The moment they notice Craig, sympathy clouds their faces. I can't handle talking to them about it, not here, maybe not for a long while. "I'm ready."

But I'm not. Not at all. Still, I grab a bag and let Craig carry the other one.

Our elevator ride to the lobby is silent. As we check out, my mind flies with all the things I want to say to Craig. Urgency and immediacy pounds in every heartbeat. But what else is there to say? *I think I'm falling for you and I wish I could stay.*

We load our bags into the waiting airport shuttle. Slater and Noah climb into the van, but I hang back. Time truly is up. I turn toward the man who unexpectedly has become more than a vacation fling. Want and longing morph into an ache in my chest.

Craig captures my hand and gently tugs me into his arms. The warmth of his chest and the strength in his hold wrap me in the most secure, sweetest embrace I've ever known. "Ty."

Arms holding him tight, I gaze into those gorgeous brown eyes. I can't say goodbye. Can't get that particular word past my lips. It seems too final. "Craig."

Behind us, the shuttle's driver clears his throat. "Sir, if we want to get you to the airport by six, we need to leave now."

Drinking in every detail of Craig's face, I press our torsos close together, determined to memorize every single thing. "Thank you for this weekend. It was unforgettable."

He brushes his lips over mine. The touch, light and sweet, is like the faintest taste of a delectable dessert that's been whipped away before I've gotten my fill.

I lick my lips, trying to hold on to the flavor of his kiss.

"I'll see you." With those words, Craig lowers his arms and then steps back. He thrusts one hand into his front pocket, lifts the other in a wave, and smiles.

The ache in my chest deepens. I return the wave and drum up a smile. Forcing myself to turn away and move my legs in the van's direction takes monumental effort, but I succeed. My hands tremble as I buckle my seatbelt. Spotlighted by the sun, Craig stands, watching, and he licks his lips like he's trying to hold on to my flavor too.

The vehicle rolls forward and gains speed. I keep my gaze on the lone silhouette until the van turns a corner, removing him from view.

"You okay?" Slater's voice breaks the silence as we merge into heavy traffic.

I shake my head. In what universe could I possibly be okay? "No. But it's time to get back to the real world."

CHAPTER SIX
CRAIG

Music echoes throughout my apartment. Head nodding to the beat of the song Patrick is playing on the acoustic guitar, I set a stack of T-shirts into one of the partially filled suitcases on the bed. Packing for the mini-tour with The Fury has kept me busy for the past hour, and I appreciate having company during the tedious task.

Sharing the stage with The Fury is a huge honor, and as soon as I knew for sure that they needed me, Ty was the first person I told. In the two weeks since the whirlwind weekend we shared, we've been texting every day, starting off by my question of how Ty's flight home had been, sent mere hours after I'd watched him drive away from the hotel.

Ty is on my mind first thing in the morning, multiple times during the day, and last thing at night. I have it bad...

Sprawled in the chair by the window, Patrick smoothly moves into the opening chords of the song we've been working on for the last few weeks. I can already imagine Cody's voice caressing the lyrics. I give him a thumbs up and turn back to my suitcase. Running through my mental checklist, I survey the contents. Jeans, shirts, socks, boxers, clothes for working out, boots, sneakers, and toiletries. And my guitar case is waiting by the front door, ready for the trip.

The strumming stops mid-way through the song. Patrick glances up from the guitar. "What time are you leaving tomorrow?"

"Luke said he'd pick me up at ten-thirty." I toss in the new notebook I purchased in case song lyrics strike, then zipper the black canvas bag closed.

"You have your phone charger?"

"Yeah, thanks." I double-check that it's still where I put it, in the front pocket of the bag holding my shoes. If I forget anything, one of the guys can probably hook me up, or with the major and mid-sized cities on the tour itinerary, buying whatever I need on the road will be easy.

I lift the suitcases. The corner of one case snags the blanket draped across the foot of the bed and tugs it halfway onto the floor. Muttering a curse, I set the cases aside and carefully fold the soft knit. Ty had used that blanket to keep warm during our night together. Every time I look at the blanket and the bed, memories of the time I spent there with him bombard me. The same holds true for my kitchen, the living room, and even the foundation's headquarters and the hospital.

Two weeks have passed, and yet, Ty's presence lingers.

Turning away from the bed, I pick up the cases once again and look at Patrick. "Want a beer?"

"Sure." He rises, starts playing again, and leads the way to the living room. The music continues as he walks, reminding me of an old-time minstrel.

The suitcases join the guitar case by the door. I lay my leather jacket on top of the bags. "Okay, I'm all set for tomorrow."

"Cool." Patrick returns the guitar to its stand. "Want me to grab the drinks?"

"I'll get them. Have a seat." With the trip so close, the fridge is pretty bare. I used up nearly all the perishables so they wouldn't go to waste. Beer and water line the fridge's bottom shelf. I snag two bottles, pop the tops, deliver them to the living room coffee table, then detour back to the kitchen to grab a container of guacamole from the fridge and a bag of tortilla chips from the counter.

When I return, Patrick lifts his beer in toast. "Food too? You rock."

"I have to use this up. And I missed lunch."

The ping of a text alert fills the air.

Adrenaline spiking through my blood, I drop the container and bag on the table and dive for my phone laying on the opposite arm of the couch. The first line of Ty's latest message fills the screen's center. A screenshot of a dragon from his portfolio lays behind it, set as my lock screen and wallpaper. He'd told me I could use it, and every time I see it, I smile.

Ty: Hey, what're you up to? I'm off to Slater's for more work on the series.

An emoji of a superhero follows his text. Grinning, I type my response. *Just finished packing for the tour. Patrick's here.*

A bubble with three blinking dots appears. I keep my gaze glued to the screen, waiting.

Ty: Have fun. Talk to you later tonight?

My thumbs fly over the keys: *I'll text you when I'm in bed.*

As soon as I hit send, that blinking dot bubble pops up beneath my message.

Ty: I'm glad you told me, now I'll know how to picture you when we're talking.

A winking face emoji appears and heat flushes into my chest. For as often as we've been chatting, we haven't exchanged particularly sexy texts yet. I have a feeling that will change very soon.

Craig: You could let me know if you'll be in bed too… So I know what to picture.

Ty: I'll send you a selfie when I get there… As long as you promise not to make fun of my superhero pajamas. :-)

I'll bet anything he looks damn cute in those. I wish I could see them on him in person tonight.

Craig: Maybe we could video chat instead of text?

Two emojis, a grinning face and a high-five, are Ty's response.

The crunching of plastic being torn open rips my attention away from my phone. I swing my gaze toward my guest.

Patrick digs into the bag of chips and emerges with a handful. "What's going on? Is that Devon or Cody? We're video chatting with them in like, ten minutes."

"No." I pause and consider how much to share. But this is Patrick, one of my oldest friends. We've never been less than honest with each other, and the man is never shy about offering his opinion or advice. "I met someone."

"Dude, that's great. I'm happy for you." He gives me a hearty slap on the back.

"He lives in Buffalo."

His brows raise, then draw together. "Oh."

"Yeah." The word holds the weight of my frustrations over Ty being all the way on the other side of the country. I set my phone facedown on the table and grab my beer. "We met at the convention two weeks ago, instantly connected, spent the entire weekend together, and have been texting a ton since he left."

"Wow. That's intense. So, are you doing the long distance thing or what?"

"I don't know." I drag a hand through my hair. "It's so new."

Nodding, my friend leans into the back cushion and crosses his legs, ankle resting on his knee. He tips back his bottle and takes a long swallow. "Then I guess you have to wait and see what happens."

"Easy for you to say." My feelings are a little too explosive for that logical brand of thinking to calm them. I stab a chip into the guac. It snaps in half.

Patrick steals the second, larger piece out of the container. "Why's that? Can't you just sit back and enjoy the ride?"

"Doing that would be easier if I knew he and I wanted to head to the same destination." My gaze flicks to my phone. The feelings I have for Ty overwhelm me. I've never had that happen before.

"Where did you get that sketch of yourself?" Beer in hand, he gestures toward the framed picture hanging on the wall over the piano.

I can't help smiling. Every time I sit down to play, my own likeness, sketched by Ty's hand, reflects back at me. "The guy I met is an artist. He sketched it the day we met."

Patrick stands, then wanders closer to the image. He tucks his hands into his back pockets as he leans in to study the sketch. "Looks just like you. He's good."

A warm mix of happiness and pride fills me, welling deep in my chest. "His name is Ty, and he's amazing. His portfolio is impressive. I'll send you a link if you want to check it out."

"Sure. I'll take a look." He strolls back to the couch. After reclaiming his seat, he studies me, his hazel gaze intense.

When he speaks again, his voice is softer, gentler. "You really like him, don't you?"

"I do." So much.

He nods. "I hope it works out the way you want."

"Thanks, man." I reach over and clink our beers together.

We dig into the chips and guacamole. Then, Patrick laughs and smacks me on the arm, dislodging a chip from my hand. His serious expression is gone, replaced by a smart ass smile. "I've never seen you so giddy over text messages."

Embarrassment wars with indignation as I brush the broken chip pieces off my lap. "I was not giddy." I *had* been smiling, that much I know. But giddy? Highly doubtful... Right?

"Buddy, which one of us had a clear view of your face?" That smile grows to a grin and he settles against the cushions, clearly enjoying himself. "If you don't like giddy, how about besotted? Smitten? Enamored? Enthralled? Beguiled?"

Laughing, I wing a chip at him, scoring a direct hit to the center of his chest. "Fuck you."

"No, thanks." His eyes gleam as his lips twist into a smirk. "I'll leave that for Ty."

"You..." Sputtering, surprised and amused, I hurl another chip. I have to give credit where it's due—Patrick is fast with a quip, and always has a witty comeback. "Bastard. But that was pretty funny."

"It was, but I can't take all the credit, you did feed me an easy setup."

"Well, I am also now *not* feeding you an actual dinner."

With a shrug like he knows my threat carries no weight, he raises his bottle to his lips. "It's probably my turn to buy anyway. Let's get the guys on video. Then we'll put in an order for food."

"Sure." I reach for my phone. Trepidation over the possibility of Ty sending another text and it popping up on the screen for Patrick to see stops me halfway. "Let's use yours instead. I'll put the pizza order in on mine."

That smart ass smile returns and Patrick slowly pulls his phone from his pocket. "I'm so onto you. But fine. I don't have anyone interesting texting me anyway."

While he opens the app and calls, I order our usual from the pizza place then clean up the chip crumbs. Cody and Devon's familiar voices fill the room. Patrick props his phone against the stack of magazines on the coffee table. He and I sprawl on opposite ends of the couch. Our friends on screen are positioned the same way, lounging in Devon's living room.

"Hey, boys." Cody beams a megawatt smile. "What's good?"

Patrick smirks and pokes his foot into my calf. "Craig met someone."

"You did?" Cody and Devon ask together, then look at each other and laugh.

Damn, I wish we were all in the same room. Settling deeper into the cushion, I pick up my beer then pass Patrick's over to him. "I did. His name is Ty. He's an artist and is deep into comic books, too."

"Ooh, he must be something." Cody leans into the screen with a sigh. The most dramatic member of our friendship quad is a total romantic. "Even your eyes are smiling."

Fingers steadily tapping out a beat on his thighs, Devon confirms Cody's words with a nod. "I'm expecting to see cartoon hearts popping out of them."

Patrick snorts a laugh, I scoff, and Cody grins.

And Devon continues with a wave of his hand, "Tell us about him."

I dive in, relaying everything that's happened since I

rescued Ty from the table disaster. My friends are enthusiastic and sympathetic, and want to see photos of Ty and of the sketch he made me, and Patrick takes too much pleasure in me needing to use my phone to accommodate their requests. Luckily, no messages pop up from Ty.

Our pizza arrives, as does Cody and Devon's. We talk, laugh, joke, and catch up on everything that's happened since our last group chat, and talk about the song we've been working on. Patrick plays the melody for them again and I share new lyrics I wrote this week. We may only occasionally put out a single, but I'll take that over nothing.

Eating the same food is almost like having them here with us like they used to be, all of us crowding around a pizza box, starving after a hard night of playing, or more often, a hard night of working shit jobs that didn't pay nearly enough. The fierceness with which I miss my friends, miss the four of us being together, hits like an unexpected punch to the solar plexus. In addition to Ty, I have two other very good reasons to make a trip to Buffalo soon.

After the call ends, I walk Patrick to the door. "We should visit the guys soon."

"And Ty?" The smirk I'm expecting of him doesn't surface.

"I hope so. I really want to see him."

He pauses with his hand on the doorknob. "We'll figure something out when you're back. Good luck with the tour. Keep me posted on how it goes. And Craig... Back to Ty, listen. I know I don't know what you're going through, but I can imagine. These next few weeks away will be busy, but I hope by the time you get back, you're closer to receiving the answer you want."

"Thanks." I hug him hard, holding on a second longer than usual. "You're a good friend."

"Keep that thought in mind if you find stray chip crumbs in the couch cushions." He's smiling as we draw apart. "See you, bud."

I lock up behind him, then turn and stare at the living room. In the absence of four voices talking over top of each other, the silence seems so loud. My gaze lands on the sketch. Then on my luggage by the door.

Maybe getting on the road for a few weeks, the change of scenery, the change of focus, will help take my mind off of the situation with Ty. Though I doubt it.

I am well and truly hooked. But if Ty ends up not wanting the same things... I lay a hand over the icy shard lodged in my stomach. If that happens... then on top of everything else, I will also be thoroughly gutted.

CHAPTER SEVEN
TY

Fighting through the floaty feeling that's been my companion thanks to working late nights with Slater, coupled with earlier than usual starts at the insurance office, I drag myself down the hallway of Slater and Noah's apartment building, thankful it's Friday. Their place is a home away from home, and for the past two weeks, I've been living here.

My sketchbook and tablet are filled with ideas and notes I jotted down during my lunch break. I'm longing for hours of uninterrupted sleep, but my level of exhaustion will have to wait, because I have a video chat scheduled with Craig in less than fifteen minutes.

One month has passed since we met. We've both been super busy, me with the two jobs and Craig on tour, yet we've managed to exchange texts every day, sometimes, multiple times a day. A month of talking, flirting, and I'm falling for him more and more.

Using the key the couple gave me, I let myself into their place, then toe off my shoes and tuck them in a corner. Slater's sneakers lay on their sides a few feet away from the wall, total tripping hazards. I push them under the small table by the front door, out of the way. "Slater?"

"In the kitchen."

Following the scent of coffee, I head that way. Slater sits at the kitchen island, his laptop open, huddled over the detailed spreadsheet we created to keep track of characters, plot lines, and scenes. I set my bag down on an empty stool and withdraw my sketchbook, tablet, and notebook. "I know we're supposed to be working, but Craig only had a small window of time to talk today, so he and I are chatting in fifteen minutes."

"No worries. Noah should be back from the library soon, and we'll need to break for dinner anyway."

"Thanks."

Sliding back his stool, Slater stands. He moves to the cabinet, takes down two mugs, then pours coffee into both. "I'm glad you're staying in touch. The chemistry you had in LA was intense. I think everyone who saw you guys picked up on it."

"Yeah." I smile and warmth washes into my chest. "He's great. I can't wait to see him."

He sets one of the cups in front of me, then retrieves cream and sugar. "When's he flying in? I can't remember what you said."

An extra teaspoon of sugar makes its way into my mug before I realize that I've already heaped in my usual amount. Hopefully, the increased sweetness will keep me going a while longer. Caffeine and sugar are the key combination for powering through the crazy hours I've been keeping lately. "His flight leaves after the concert on Friday night. There's a layover in Chicago, so he's due to get here at eleven-thirty next Saturday morning."

"You seem happier since you met him."

"I am." I take a sip of the brew and my gaze falls to my notebook and the ideas that sparked into my head during lunch. "Craig is amazing. He's sweet, sexy, smart, and kind. I feel like I'm trapped under his spell, which gave me an idea for the next hero we're planning. I want to do something like that. Craig is all-consuming, and I can't get enough. But I don't know whether that should be in our hero's favor or detriment."

His head tips to the side as he studies me. "I like it, and can picture either route working well. We can discuss the pros and cons during dinner, and I'll show you the storyboard I played with today before we dive into more work."

"Good plan." And maybe we'll finish at an early enough hour that I'll get a decent amount of sleep.

Slater glances at the microwave clock. "Are you taking your call in your bedroom? Or did you want to do it out here? I can make myself scarce."

"It's your apartment. You don't have to hide away. I'll go in the guest room." Carrying my coffee, phone, and sketchbook, I head for the room I've been sleeping in for the past two weeks. They've both christened it my bedroom rather than calling it the guest room, and not for the first time, I wish I had the pair as roommates for real.

I change my shirt, comb my hair, and choose the chair by the window instead of the bed. If I lay down, the chance I'll fall asleep is too great.

A few short minutes later, Craig fills my screen. Shirtless, lounging on a bed, propped up against a pile of pillows, he smiles and his eyes crinkle at the corners. "Hey."

Just seeing his face on the screen is enough to brighten my world. "Hi. You look good, all sprawled out like that."

"You do too, with the light playing over your face. And I bet you feel even better. I wish you were here."

"Me too." I hide a yawn behind my coffee mug. "How was last night's show?"

The purple shadows under his dark gaze are deeper than when we video chatted last week. "The crowd was great. Tons of energy. But I'm exhausted."

He still has one week to go. I stifle another yawn. "I hope you're taking care of yourself. Staying hydrated. Eating as nutritiously as possible."

"I am." Craig's image zooms in on his face as he brings his phone closer to it. His brows draw together. "You look really tired. Just like last week."

"It's all the hours we've been pulling on the comic book series, coupled with going into work early for training on how to use the new software and claims system this week." I don't think the company should be allowed to schedule training sessions outside of our normal working hours, but the higher ups don't care, so I'm using my frustration as fuel to push harder on the comics.

Craig's brows lower and his chin raises. He tilts his head and seems to be choosing his words carefully. "Even though you're creating superheroes, remember, *you're* still human. Don't overdo it."

Knowing he cares gives me a soft and cozy feeling. "I'll do my best. You should take your own advice. Hanging out with that big rock band famous for getting into problems, like bar fights..." I'm not kidding, but soften my warning with a smile.

"They've mellowed out over the last several years. I think starting Furious Records was a turning point for them. No fights or problems this tour. Even Zander's in a decent mood, considering he still can't play without pain."

I wince in sympathy. "I hope he's better soon. A few years ago, I sprained two fingers and couldn't properly grip a pencil for two weeks. That's the longest I've ever gone without drawing. I hated every minute."

He shifts his position and adjusts the pillow. "How'd you sprain them?"

"I was getting out of bed and my legs got tangled in the sheets. I fell forward, hit the floor, and bent the fingers back too far."

With a grimace, Craig turns his head away from the screen. "Ouch."

"Yeah. Took even longer before I got my full range of motion back. I'm lucky it wasn't worse." I fight another yawn, but fail to hold it off.

Lines of concern etch across his face. "You keep yawning. I should let you go so you can rest."

"No!" Clutching my coffee, I widen my eyes and do my best to look wide awake. The adrenaline shooting through my system at the thought of the call being severed helps, as does gulping half of the coffee. "I want to talk to you. I've looked forward to this all day. Stay. Please. It's only some missed sleep. No big deal."

"Yeah, it's *only* something your body needs to function properly. No big deal," he mocks gently. "If you go for something like fifty hours without sleep, you can start hallucinating."

"Are you speaking from experience?"

Craig's rich chuckle flows from the speakers. "Just something I read recently."

"I did some interesting reading, too. Today, actually, during my lunch break. On narwhals."

"Oh?"

"I was thinking about your tattoo. Sketching it out. So I looked them up. Did you know, some people call them the unicorn of the sea because of the tusk?"

"Makes sense." He glances at the colorful tattoo adorning his biceps. "I told you I don't remember picking this out, so I don't know how I ended up with it over something else, or why, in my inebriated state, I thought permanently inking this onto my skin was a great idea."

Sympathy swirling, I shift closer to the screen, wishing I could somehow allay Craig's discomfort. "Maybe it's time to consider covering the tattoo with something else? Something that will make you happy. If you want, I could draw something for you. I've designed tattoos for one of my coworkers and for Noah."

Light comes into his eyes and Craig beams. "I could be walking around with a piece of art, a Typhoeus Allen original, on my arm?"

"I like when you put it that way." Stretching out my legs, I savor this talented man's appreciation of my work, and the way it makes me feel buzzed, like the most potent drink. "I can draw whatever you want."

"I really like that first dragon you have in your portfolio. The one I'm using as a lock screen. Maybe something like that?"

Fingers itching to get started, I set the coffee on the windowsill and grab the sketchbook. "Definitely. Think about colors you want, the feel of the dragon. How big? Will it be flying? Breathing fire? Breathing music notes? Have music notes etched into its scales?"

"I love the way your mind works. Definitely yes to music notes."

My pencil scratches over the paper as I jot down some thoughts. "I'll play with some ideas and send them to you."

"I can't wait to see them. Send me an invoice too. I don't know the going rate for this sort of thing. Whatever you charge works for me."

My pencil pauses, mid-word. "You don't have to pay me. It was my idea, and I'm happy to do it for you."

"You are *not* working for free." The lift to his chin dares me to argue. "I've seen some of the comments under your social media posts, so I know too many people already ask for things and want them for free. That isn't right. I'm paying."

He's not wrong about those people. "Okay. I'll send an invoice once we finalize the design. That's how I've done it with Noah."

Craig gives one sharp nod. "Deal." And we grin at each other.

Sunshiny warmth radiates through me, and I long to bask in the glow for as long as he'll have me. Craig makes me so happy. Is this love? Is this too soon to be love? I want what is best for the man, want him to be safe and content. And I want to be my best self for him too. But saying all of that only one month into knowing him could scare him off. It's too soon to share. Way too soon. There's still so much up in the air. I settle on a safe topic instead. The saga of his hotel room experiences up and down California. "How's your hotel room?"

"The A/C's working, so it's already better than the last place. And there's a piano in the lobby, which is cool. Remember the ballad I played for you? I played it for the guys earlier. They asked if I'd go into the studio and record it with them after the tour's over."

"That's amazing. Ask them if you can sing too. Your voice is so good."

Craig's head dips, and that almost shy look he'd worn while playing the song reappears. "They heard me today. Luke said he wants us to do it together as a duet."

Pride in Craig puffs up my chest and I pump my arm into

the air. "Yes! I can't wait to hear it. Of course, hearing it in person, with you right next to me was really special. Like my own private concert."

"Speaking of in person and private." He shifts his position, rustling the sheets as he turns onto his side. "I know we'd planned for me to hop on a flight after the last show and come see you."

"Yes, and I can't wait." My heart skips and my pulse jumps at the thought of having him here with me for a few days of uninterrupted togetherness. I shift forward in the chair. My sketchbook and pencil slide off my lap, and I scramble to catch them before they tumble to the floor. "I already cleared it with my roommates and we'll be finished the training on the new system at work next week, so I won't have to worry about putting in extra hours while you're here."

His expression a mix of hesitation and stress, Craig drags his hand through his hair. "Thing is, the guys want to get into the studio on Monday next week, fresh off the tour, to do the recording."

"Oh."

He's not coming.

A lead weight forms in my stomach. I set the pencil down to mark my place and close the sketchbook. The sunlight filtering through the window dims, casting the room in shadows as the sun slips behind clouds. "I understand."

"I hate cancelling on you." His voice draws my focus back to the screen. Creases fan out in fine lines from the corners of his eyes and he licks his lips. "I'm really sorry."

"I'm disappointed, but it's okay." Disappointed is an understatement. I'm a few notches below painful. But I don't want to tell him that when he looks like he feels bad enough. "Recording that song is a great opportunity."

Craig's sigh is so heavy a forklift wouldn't be able to raise it. "It is. But I want to see you. I could still fly out late Friday night as planned. Arrive in Buffalo at eleven-thirty on Saturday morning. And take the eleven AM flight back to LA on Sunday."

"I want to see you. But I couldn't do that to you, not with you having to sing and be ready to record on Monday. You should spend the weekend at home, resting and relaxing."

"Twenty-four hours together is better than nothing."

Now, it's my turn to sigh. "I agree. But, you're exhausted already. Spending tons of hours stuck on planes and in airports in such a short span of time will only make that worse." My stomach tightens. "I don't want you blaming me if you're at less than your best on Monday."

With his frown, the intensity in his gaze burns brighter. "Hold on. Why would I blame you?"

The best answer I can manage is a shrug. Instances of my parents' remarks about missing out on things because of "the kid" aren't something I dwell on, but the feelings associated with them tend to surface at odd times and catch me unaware. "Just thinking."

Craig holds my gaze, unmoving. Unblinking. Studying me, and I fear he sees too deeply. "Too much passed over your face. Tell me what you're thinking about that would make you believe I'd blame you."

Silence stretches out between us as I gather my thoughts. Discomfort tickling along my spine, I hook my ankle around the chair's rung. "Let's just say I've heard the same thing often enough, drawing that conclusion is almost natural."

His brows knit together. "Not Slater and Noah."

"No. Not them. My parents. They had me really young, and a baby was *not* in their plans. We lived with my grandparents so they could watch me while my parents worked part-time around their college classes. My grandparents hadn't planned on the three of us interrupting their lives for so many years. As I heard them say more than once, they already raised their kids and didn't feel up to doing it again, which I understood. But my parents didn't want to do it either."

"I'm sorry." His voice is soft.

A chill creeping over my skin, I fold my legs up against my chest and shift toward the slowly forming sunbeam filtering through the window. "My grandparents are gone now. I don't have a relationship with my parents. I got tired of hearing how I was the reason their lives didn't turn out the way they'd planned."

Craig sighs and shifts, tucking one arm behind his head on the pillow. "I hate when people blame others for situations they put themselves in. I'm sorry you went through that. So sorry."

I don't know what to say, so I nod.

He pulls his phone closer to his face and his gaze is serious, locked in on mine. "Let's be clear. If I choose to do or not do something, that is on me. I don't blame other people for my actions and reactions."

The words soak in, soothing old wounds. "Noted."

"Good."

I really don't want to argue with him, and as much as I want him in my arms, putting aside what I want is the right thing to do. "I still think you should stay in LA and get some rest. Please? For me?"

Softness flickers in his eyes. He rubs his hand over his face, and when he focuses back on the screen, I can see his resolve has weakened. "Saying I'd do anything for you isn't much of an exaggeration."

That surprises me. And makes me hope. And realize there isn't much I wouldn't do for him. "Same here."

The softness continues in the smile shaping his lips. "Good to know."

My gaze falls on the color-coded calendar of comic book tasks I printed out, poking from the sketchbook. "Slater and I still have more to do to prepare for our launch. So while you're in the recording booth, I can focus on that."

A line forms between his brows. "I thought you said you were ahead of schedule."

"I am." Busting my ass and getting things squared away so I'd have time for Craig put me there. "But we're almost done. The only other thing I have on my calendar is the party Noah is giving us on launch day to celebrate our series going live. You're welcome to come."

He nods. "I want to be there, celebrating with you. I have meetings with a few artists later this month to talk about songs they want. Maybe I can fly out after those are finished. Come to the party. Stay for a while."

New tendrils of hope bloom and unfurl, though the wisps are thin and difficult to grasp. "I'd love that."

"I'll do my best to make it happen." Incessant beeping interrupts his voice. His muscles flex as he leans over the mattress and silences the alarm clock. "Sorry, but I need to get going. The band has an interview."

I bite my lip to hold back saying I'd hoped we'd have a longer time together. "I'll talk to you soon."

"Don't overwork yourself."

Despite the pit in my stomach, I manage a smile and lift my hand in a wave. "Right. I won't. You either."

The spark twinkling in his gaze at the call's start isn't as bright now. He brings his fingers to his lips, then his hand comes forward, to the screen. Almost like a kiss goodbye. And then his screen goes black.

Unsettled, I stare at the phone, replaying our conversation. Exhaustion limits my brain from firing on all cylinders. Everything feels muddy and uncertain. I'm afraid to get my hopes up that he'll be able to attend the party. Something else could come up, like another gig. He's already had another band reach out to see if he could join them for a special project and the details for that are up in the air.

I fight through another yawn and stand. My socked feet shuffling across the wood floors, I return to the kitchen. The oven is on and the scent of roasted chicken and potatoes fills the air. The papers and laptop still clutter the island, but Slater's coffee cup and the man himself are gone. A peek into the hall confirms Slater and Noah's bedroom door is closed. The stack of library books by the couch means Noah is home. He's probably in the bedroom, changing clothes, with Slater keeping him company.

A wave of exhaustion washes over me once again. Clutching the island's edge, I squeeze hard, willing it to pass. Another massive yawn overtakes me.

Despite the tiredness and the stress over Craig, I have work to do. I open the drawing app on my tablet. The superhero I created dominates the screen. Pencil in hand, I pause over the panel, unable to concentrate on his battle with the villain. My thoughts fly back to Craig.

The sound of a door opening is followed by Slater and Noah's voices, then footsteps in the hallway. They enter the kitchen. Noah meets my gaze and stops in his tracks. "You look upset."

"I'm okay." I glance at my coffee cup, debating another refill.

"No you're not," Slater says, crossing his arms over his chest. He moves toward me like a bodyguard intent on providing protection. "How was the call with Craig?"

Shrugging, I push off the stool. "All right. Well, no. Let's change that to not the best."

Noah and Slater exchange a glance, and Noah inclines his head before continuing to the fridge. He removes carrots, celery, lettuce, and a yellow pepper, then places them next to the tomato resting on the counter. "What happened?"

I shove my hands into my back pockets and pace from one side of the room to the other, studying the pattern in the wood grain. "The band asked him to record a song with them as soon as the tour ends. So he can't come for a visit like we'd planned. That's getting pushed back for a while."

"I'm sorry." Noah's voice is as soft as the comforting hand he lays on my shoulder.

I wish ditching my disappointment was as easy as releasing a breath or rolling my shoulders. But instead, it lingers, as gray as the clouds forming in the sky outside the window. "We're busy working on the comic anyway, and he has some work lined up later this month, so I guess waiting might be smarter for us. He said he'd try to be here for our launch party."

Slater plucks my coffee cup from the counter and brings it to the pot. "I'm sorry his visit got postponed. We know you were looking forward to it."

The dark brew flows into our cups, and the rich scent drifts on the air. Inhaling deep, I drag my hands through my hair. "He offered to fly out anyway, but we'd only have about twenty-four hours together between his flights. I can't put him through all the waiting at airports and being stuck cramped in a seat on those long flights for hours and hours. He needs to be at his best for recording."

He sets the coffee in front of me, along with the cream and sugar. "What if you went to see him? I know you said you don't have any vacation time left at the day job this year, but you could go for the weekend. Fly out on Friday late afternoon or evening and fly home on Sunday night. It's not a ton of time together, but you won't have to worry about him dealing with the airports and flights."

Stirring in the sugar, I watch the swirling liquid. "That's a nice idea. Maybe in a few months."

I need to wait until I've rebuilt my bank account, replacing the money I spent on the trip to LA. As professional hockey players, the amount of money Slater and Noah earn is so high above what I make it's not funny, though they never flaunt that fact or make things awkward.

Noah picks up his laptop from where it rests on the side counter. "You said Craig's last show is in LA?"

I pass Slater the container of creamer. "Yeah. The band has shows there Thursday and Friday. They booked hotel rooms so they don't have to worry about driving home in between shows. But he'll be back in his house on Saturday."

"Cool. Then that's where you'll be." Slater lays his hand on my shoulder. "Our treat."

Shaking my head, I back away, whipping my gaze from him to Noah. "No. I can't let you do that."

"Sure you can. We want to." Busy typing and clicking away, Noah gives me a brief glance before returning his focus to the screen. I spy the website of the airline we used when flying to LA for the convention. "You're helping Slater realize his dream of having the comic book series come to life. That's huge, Ty. We both appreciate you."

"Yeah, but that project is helping me. Slater brings great ideas and an audience. And you two have been so good to me." I doubt I'll ever be able to thank them for welcoming me into their lives and giving me a place in their circle of friends, not to mention that most of my friends now have come from knowing the pair. They've changed my life.

Noah steps back from his laptop and faces me, placing his hands on my shoulders. "We're friends. We can do things for each other. Now, I've booked the flights. You fly out Friday afternoon at four o'clock. The return flight is Sunday night at six-thirty. Direct flights, no layovers. We can take you to and from the airport so you don't have to worry about leaving your car, or dealing with ordering a rideshare. Since you're staying here anyway, it makes the most sense."

Overwhelmed, I clutch hold of his wrist. "I don't know what to say. Thank you doesn't seem like enough, but thank you."

Slater joins us and slips his arm around Noah's waist. The pair lean into each other, fitting perfectly. "You're a good guy, Ty. We've got your back."

"I know you do." They've more than proven so. I'll have to think of something nice to repay them.

"Good." Noah releases his hold, then beckons me toward the island and the mess of papers. "The chicken and potatoes will be ready by the time we finish chopping up the salad veggies. They're already cooked, I picked them up on the way home. We're just reheating."

I gather the sheets into a pile. "I'll help with the chopping. And I can set the table."

Slater grins at me. "For a supervillain fan, you're awfully conscientious about helping out."

Laughing, I chuck a balled-up piece of paper at his chest. "What can I say? Like the best villains, I'm a complex character."

The guys crack up, and I join in. I can't wait to tell Craig I'm coming out to see him. I'm itching to call him now, but I don't want to interrupt the band's interview.

An entire day and a half with Craig sounds like another whirlwind, and I can't wait to get swept up in it.

CHAPTER EIGHT
CRAIG

Steam from my shower fills the bathroom, fogging the mirror. I rush through toweling off, then dig out jeans, boxers, and a T-shirt from my suitcase. The adrenaline from spending the past two hours on stage thrums through me, feeding into the electric charge of knowing Ty will be here, in my suite and in my arms, tonight.

When he called me with the news that his friends gifted him the flights to come see me, I was over the moon happy. It's something I'd considered doing myself, and if this goes the way I hope it will, I'll be more than happy to pay for future flights if he'll let me.

My phone chimes with a text alert as I slide on my boxers. I snatch it up and find two messages. The newest is from Luke, above one from Ty that came in while I showered.

Ty: I'm at the airport and waiting for a taxi. See you soon.

Luke: Hey bud, we're in the lounge on the tenth floor tonight if you and your man feel like joining us. Private party, just us and the road crew. Otherwise, we'll see you on Monday.

I love hanging out with the band, but tonight is all about

Ty. They were cool about me rushing off after the last song so I could get back here and get myself ready. In a lot of ways, they remind me of my best friends. A tight knit group, its own family, friendships forged through highs and hardships.

Three rapid knocks sound at the door. My pulse racing, I tug on my shirt then jeans, zipping up as I hurry toward it. Ty's here already? I look through the peephole.

Cody, Devon, and Patrick are crowded in the hallway.

What the hell?

I flip the locks, then tug the door open. Three smiling faces greet me. "Guys? What are you doing here?"

"Surprise!" Cody flings his arms around me, full of enthusiasm, squeezing me so tight breathing is difficult. "We came to see you in action. You were awesome, such a great show."

Wearing a hoodie with the Buffalo Bedlam's logo at the center of his chest, Devon hugs me next. He's the shortest of our group, though Cody only has an inch or so on him. "Patrick got us tickets for tonight's show."

Patrick brings up the rear, clad in a leather jacket and clutching a bottle of water. "I texted Luke once we knew for sure that you were still filling in for Zander tonight and asked him, said we wanted to surprise you."

My first bandmates and oldest, closest friends pile into my room. The four of us are together in the same place again, after several months of being apart. I let the door swing shut and follow them into the suite. "Well, you did. I can't believe you're here."

Cody drops onto the bed with enough force to bounce. "It's not every day our friend gets to play with a multi-platinum band. I wanted to come out and support you earlier in the tour, but couldn't get time off work until now. Still, we made it for your last show. I'm so proud of you."

"You looked good up there," Patrick adds, sitting beside

Cody. "Luke gave us your room number. I was hoping we'd get to the arena for the pre-show meet and greet, but Cody and Devon's flight was delayed. We arrived right before The Fury took the stage."

"I'm glad we got to close out the tour with you." Devon's smile is beaming, pride for me shining in his eyes. "You ready for it to be over?"

Patrick narrows his eyes at me. "You look exhausted."

"Yeah. I am. But I'll have tomorrow and Sunday to decompress. On Monday, we're recording that song at Zander's home studio." I peek at my phone, but Ty hasn't sent any new messages. "Listen, Ty's on his way."

"What, here? Now?" Devon asks.

"He texted me a little while ago from the airport. He was waiting for a taxi. He'll be here until Sunday afternoon."

Cody's eyes grow wide. He looks at Devon, then me, then hits Patrick in the stomach with the back of his hand. "We got to see you in your rock star glory *and* we get to meet Ty? This visit just keeps getting better."

Patrick lays his hand on Cody's thigh to stifle his movements. "You're making me seasick with all that flailing around."

Ignoring the pair, Devon rubs his hand over the back of his neck as he settles onto a chair near the window. "Sorry we're ruining your reunion with Ty. Maybe we shouldn't have shown up here without any warning."

"Sorry, Craig. The surprise part was my idea." Cody winces and regret dulls the excited shine in his eyes.

I've really missed these guys, and wish I could clone myself so I could spend as much time as possible with both them and Ty without anyone feeling left out. "It's good to see you. I'm glad you're here."

"I wish we could stay longer. Cody and I are flying home

on Monday night. I have to be back at work for inventory on Tuesday." Devon stretches his arms overhead, then cracks his neck from side to side. An avid runner, he manages a shop that sells running gear and pairs runners from beginner to advanced levels with coaches and training programs.

A knock on the door sends my heartbeat skyrocketing, and we all stand. Weaving past Cody and Patrick, I head for the door. The peephole shows Ty standing in the hall, like sunshine himself, wearing a bright yellow T-shirt and jeans. "He's here."

My pulse pounding, I open the door. Ty standing before me is almost surreal. I keep thinking about when we had to say goodbye that morning at his hotel, and how I didn't want him getting on that plane. "You made it. You're really here."

His smile grows bigger and brighter. "Hi."

Aching to pull him into my arms, I don't want to begin our reunion in a hallway, so I step back and swing the door open wide. "Come in. Meet my friends."

"Friends?" His smile dims as surprise overtakes his features. Hiking his travel bag higher on his shoulder, Ty slips past me, but doesn't venture farther than a few feet beyond the entryway. The view of the rest of the room is hidden by the narrow mini-hall created by the bathroom and closet.

"Old friends. They flew in to surprise me."

"Oh." His hand tightens around the strap of his bag, and he bites his lip. His gaze darts from the hallway to his sneakers and then lands on my eyes. "Your old bandmates? I…"

He's all vibrating nerves, and I am, too. I slip my hand to the small of his back and pull him into my chest. The travel bag hits my side as he wraps his arms around my torso.

Holding him feels as good as before.

Having him here, holding him again, how tight he's

clinging to me, I'm bombarded with longing, relief, satisfaction, and desire. He lifts his face to mine. After weeks of seeing him through a phone screen, I get to touch him, to feel that soft skin under my stroking fingers, and gaze into those light brown eyes. "Damn, it's good to see you."

Leaning into my hand cupping his cheek, he nods and his trembling fingers fan out on my upper back and flex, then shift higher to grasp my shoulders. "You too. It's silly to say that I missed you since we chat all the time, but I did."

"I did, too." The urge to kiss him pulses with every heartbeat. Sliding my hand into his hair, I bend my head. His tongue peeks out to wet his lips, then he smiles and pulls me the rest of the way down.

His lips are warm and soft, and I draw his scent into my lungs. That overwhelmed feeling crashes through me once more.

He's here. In my arms. And damn, he feels so good.

His hands roam my back, the strength in his arms keeping us banded together. Ty opens for me, allowing me to deepen the kiss, and with a groan, presses against me, matching me with the same eagerness and passion.

"Aw, look at them. So sweet." Cody's whisper reminds me there are three people waiting to meet Ty.

Ty's short hairs tickle my palm as my hand journeys from the back of his head to rest at the nape of his neck. With one last brush of my lips against his, I raise my head. Gaze misty, Ty smiles at me. The tight hold he has on my shoulders eases, and his fingers graze along the sides of my torso like he's reluctant to lose contact. His travel bag slips off his shoulder and hits the floor with a thud.

"Come meet the guys." Keeping my arm around him, I guide him down the short hall to the large room. Patrick and Cody are again lounging on the bed and Devon has moved from the chair to the couch. "Guys, this is Ty. Ty, that's Patrick, Cody, and Devon."

Cody is the first to stand, bouncing from his spot to embrace Ty. "So good to meet you."

"You too." If Ty's taken aback by the enthusiastic embrace, he doesn't let on. Released from Cody, he shakes hands with Patrick, then Devon. My friends reclaim their spots. Standing at the foot of Cody and Patrick's bed, Ty glances at the other empty bed, then the desk chair, then the couch, and then me.

Lacing my fingers through his, I gently pull him to the side of the free bed, and we both sit. He presses his thigh against mine as though he can't get close enough. I hope he's not intimidated or overwhelmed by the guys. The nerves over how things would be when Ty and I came face to face have now shifted into anxiousness over how everyone will get along and if they'll all like each other. My skin feeling too tight, I roll my shoulders. "I hadn't expected your paths to cross so soon. But I'm glad you all have the chance to meet."

Cody leans forward with a friendly smile. "We've heard a lot about you from Craig, Ty."

"Including how he saved me from crashing headfirst into a concrete floor?" Brown eyes shining, Ty presses his shoulder into mine. "All I saw was the costume and for a second thought I was being rescued by a real life superhero. And I was right."

Chuckling, I settle our joined hands on my thigh and press a kiss to his shoulder. "Of all the booths in all the comic book conventions in the world, I'm just glad you crashed into mine."

"Me too." His hand tightens around mine and his smile blooms. Then he drags his gaze away from me and focuses on my friends. "Craig's told me about you all too. I know Devon is your group athlete. Congrats on finishing your last marathon with such a good time, by the way." He pauses while Devon gives him a look that is both surprised and pleased. "And Cody, I hear you're a social media genius, and that you maintain the band's profiles and website."

Cody beams at me, then Ty. "I don't know about genius, but yeah, I do handle that for our band."

The tight grip Ty has on me eases as he turns to Patrick. "And Patrick, Craig told me how much he valued your help on that last song he wrote when he was up against his deadline."

A faint flush colors Patrick's cheeks. He shifts his body and shrugs, as though his assistance wasn't the eleventh-hour lifesaver we both know it to be. "What he already had gave us a great foundation to work with."

"You are way too modest, man." I raise my eyebrow, holding Patrick's gaze until he smirks and nods at me, then turn to Ty, tracing a knuckle under his chin. The purple shadows under his eyes are much lighter than they'd been on our video call. "Did you get some sleep on the flight?"

"I slept through most of it. Slater got me noise-canceling headphones and Noah gave me a neck pillow that helped a lot."

Cody snatches a pillow from the head of the bed and hugs it to his chest. "Slater's your comic book partner, right? Craig said he's a member of the Buffalo Bedlam. Devon loves hockey. He's a big Bedlam fan."

Ty twists toward Devon, his eyebrows raising in interest. "Yeah? Slater Knox is working on the series with me. I stay with him and Noah Alzado a lot. They're really good guys. I didn't watch hockey at all before I met them, but since we've become friends and I've gotten to know a few of their teammates, I guess you could say I've become a fan of the sport. Though I only watch Bedlam games."

Devon's fingers tangle in the blue drawstring hanging from his hoodie. For the first time since his arrival, I notice there's a player's number printed below the team's logo, and yep, it's Anton Celek, the team captain's number. "Have you met Anton Celek? He's my favorite player."

Ty fully relaxes against my side. He draws up one leg, tucking it underneath the other, and I catch a glimpse of the side of his sock, imprinted with tiny superhero symbols. "Celek's really nice. Laid back. Always looking out for his friends. I see him about once a month with the other guys at the team's book club meetings."

"It's cool that they post the book so the Bedlam fans can read along too. I've been a part of it since the beginning." Devon drums his fingers along the side of his thigh, his gaze darting to his phone. "Celek's pick last month was great. That mystery kept me guessing until the end."

"Whoever chooses the book hosts the meeting, so we were at his apartment for that one. His book collection is huge. It takes up an entire room. He's great about lending out the books. I'll have to tell him I met someone wearing his number."

"Is he single?" Propping another pillow behind his back, Cody keeps his attention on Ty. "Inquiring minds, and certain drummers with an affinity for running, *ahem* Devon, want to know."

I snort, completely unsurprised that Cody would ask. Cody, Patrick, and I have known about Devon's crush for a while. When watching a game with him, his attention always strays to Celek whether the captain is on the ice or the bench.

Caught in the crossroad of Devon's blushing stammer and Cody's unrepentant grin, Ty leans into me like he's seeking reassurance. "As far as I know, yes. He was dating someone back when I met Slater, but that ended a while ago."

Patrick swipes the pillow from Cody's lap and stuffs it behind his own back. "Stop trying to play matchmaker for Devon."

Cody makes a grab for the pillow's edge, his fingers digging into the fluffy white cloud. "Why? Devon's amazing. Anyone would be lucky to have him. Stop being a killjoy, Paddy."

"Don't call me that." The words grunt out through clenched teeth.

Cody rolls his eyes, releasing his hold of the pillow. "You love it."

"Anyone want to get a drink at the bar?" Devon asks too brightly, sending a quelling look to Cody and Patrick. If left to their own devices, the pair will bicker all night.

"I do." Patrick stands, throws the pillow at Cody, who catches it, falling onto his back.

"Me too." Punching an arm into the air, Cody sits up and smiles at Ty. " Let's go. We have *so* many stories about Craig."

Amusement lights Ty's face. He squeezes my hand, then presses a kiss to my cheek before standing. "That sounds like fun."

Rubbing my hands over my face, I hold back my sigh. Nothing about tonight is going as planned. Might as well roll with it. "Luke said the guys are in the lounge on the tenth floor and we're welcome to join them."

Patrick extends a hand to Cody to help pull him to his feet. As quick as they are to fight, the tension fades just as fast. "He sent a text with that invite to me, too. It's been a while since I spent any time with Luke, and longer for the other guys. Seeing them again will be cool."

"Great, let's go." Cody hooks his arm through Ty's. "We're so excited you're here."

He leads the way to the door. I shove my feet into my sneakers, pocket my wallet and room card, then follow my friends and Ty into the hall. Ty drops back to wait for me, a smile in his eyes, and his hand finds mine like we've spent a lifetime reaching for each other.

The urge to pull him into me and run my hands over every inch of him, soaking up his words and scent is strong, but with the guys here, I can't close us off in a private bubble like I want. Stroking my thumb over a patch of skin by his knuckle, I keep him close, answering my friends' questions about the show as we take the elevator to the tenth floor.

Two of the band's security guards stand like sentries on opposite sides of the lounge's door. They allow us through. Several members of the band's crew are at the tables, couches, and chairs throughout the room. Luke and Zander sit at a nearby couch. Brendan and Landry are by the bar.

Luke sees us, and a smile lights up his face as he stands and waves us over. "Hey, look who's all here. Drinks and food are on us tonight." He pulls Patrick in for a hug. "It's been too long, man."

"Good to see you. Thanks for helping us out with the tickets." Patrick hugs Zander next, then steps back and gestures to our friends. "Luke and Zander, this is Devon. And Cody." They both shake hands with the pair. He then gestures to Ty. "And this is Ty."

Zander shakes Ty's hand first. "Good to meet you."

"You too. I'm a big fan of the band."

Luke's smile widens. His gaze flicks to mine before he turns his focus on Ty and clasps his hand. "I've heard a lot about you, Ty. Craig's been looking forward to your visit."

His cheeks flushing, Ty presses his shoulder into mine. "I've been looking forward to it, too."

"Sit. Relax. Plenty of room for everyone." Luke points to the couch and chairs grouped around a long, low table. "Patrick, I forgot to tell you, I was cleaning out boxes from the garage before the tour and found an old recording of you and me."

Patrick drops onto the chair closest to Luke. "No way. What song?"

"*Don't Stop Me Now*. The best duet to come out of that nightmare experience."

Chuckling, he rubs his hand over his jaw. "I'd love to get a copy of that."

I spy Ty's questioning gaze and with a tug on his hand, pull him onto the couch with me. "Luke and Patrick were briefly in a band together years ago."

Nodding, Luke shifts over so Zander and Devon can sit beside him. "Why don't you come over tomorrow? I'll make you a copy. Hell, we can sing it right there in my studio. Jam a bit. I'd love that. We'll have a cookout too." He casts his gaze over all of us. "You're all welcome to join us."

Cody perches on the arm of Patrick's chair. "The chance to hear Paddy sing? I'm in."

Eyes warm, Luke gestures to Cody with his bottle of beer. "I hope I get to hear you sing too, man. From what I've heard in your songs, you have a hell of a range."

With a squeak, a wide-eyed Cody slips off the chair's arm and onto Patrick's lap. "You've... heard us?"

"I've followed your band from the beginning. You have a great sound. My home studio isn't as big as Zander's, but it's still decent. I'd love to jam with you."

"I want to hear the two of you sing together. You both have such powerful voices." Zander tips his glass at the guys.

"And Devon, I watched the drum solo you did during your cover of *Cut Down*. Brendan and I were blown away. I want to see that in person, if you'll play for us."

"Holy shit." Cody clutches Patrick's hand. "Craig. Paddy. Devon. I can't believe this is happening." His low voice, filled with awe, stirs goosebumps on my skin. Playing together for an audience of rock royalty is a huge deal.

With a cough and a run of his hands through his hair, Devon attempts to school the surprise stealing over his features. "Sounds fun. It would be an honor to jam with you."

Patrick shifts Cody's weight to his other thigh. "I'm in."

I open my mouth, but hesitation holds my words back. Wanting to take part, to see what it's like with these two groups existing in the same space wars with wanting time with Ty.

Ty squeezes my hand and smiles in understanding. "I'd love to see you all play together."

Luke sits back with a satisfied smile. "Great. It's settled. Once Brendan and Landry get back, we'll loop them in."

"Are you sure?" Murmuring the question close to Ty's ear, I steal a kiss to his temple. "We don't have to go."

He presses against me. "Yeah. Definitely. I want to."

A waitress arrives for our drink orders, then Landry and Brendan join us and set off a second round of introductions. My friends fall into conversations with the band, chatting away like they've known each other for years. Devon and Brendan are side by side, their attention held by a video of a drum solo on Brendan's phone. Landry and Patrick look like twins in their leather jackets, discussing a guitarist they both idolized growing up. And Cody's animated recount of one of our earliest shows has Zander and Luke in stitches. I'm relieved, though not surprised they're getting along so well.

Keeping my hands off Ty is impossible. I wrap one arm around his waist, hugging him, and he relaxes into me, laying a hand atop mine to keep me close. We chat about our week and he shows me some of the new artwork he completed for the comic book series. The connection we share feels electric and necessary, completing me in a way I didn't realize I was missing until I saw him again. It's also huge and scary and breathtaking. I never want it to end.

In between trading teasing remarks with each other, Cody, Patrick, and Devon entertain Ty with stories about me. The Fury members add in a few more, and I swing from amused to slightly embarrassed to laughing so hard I can barely breathe. I can only hope I'll have the chance to do this with Ty someday, with his friends in Buffalo.

He tips his head onto my shoulder and his eyes twinkle with his smile. "I feel like I know you so much better now."

"I hope that's a good thing." Affection for him swells from deep in my chest. The way we are with each other feels so natural and he fits in with my friends like he's been a part of us all along.

The brush of his thumb on the side of my hand is hypnotic. "A very good thing."

"Hey, Ty. I have photos of Craig from our early gigs." Cody waves his phone. "Come see."

"I can't pass that up." With a kiss to my cheek, he slips from my arms, then joins Cody on the chair.

Cody's album of band pics is huge and will take them some time to look through. I take the opportunity to move to the bar and order another drink.

Devon joins me and puts in his order, then leans on the bar, bumping his shoulder into mine. "Ty seems like a good guy. I'm happy for you."

My gaze lingers on my blond-haired man. "Being with him is like being given something I've been yearning for. But we live on opposite sides of the country. It's still early."

"Mmm hmm." Devon bumps my shoulder again. "I saw the way you lit up when he arrived. How you are with him. That's something special."

"It is. He is. But I don't know where anything will lead."

"Sorry again about interrupting your reunion. If we'd known, we wouldn't have shown up tonight."

"Don't worry about it. Good of you guys to come out." I pause while the bartender sets out two new bottles and clears away the empties. "It's a great surprise, Dev. I'm happy to see you."

"You performing with The Fury is a big deal." He taps his bottle against mine. "We wanted to support you."

Leaning an elbow on the bar, I turn to face the room. "I wasn't sure how I'd feel, being back up there, playing live for people night after night. If I'd want it again. I'm happy to be helping out my friends. It's fun. Exhausting too. But it's not the same as having the three of you up there beside me."

Wistfulness mists through his gaze. He takes a long pull of his beer. "I miss that too. Sometimes, I wonder what would've happened if I hadn't gone back to Buffalo."

"I do, too." I hate that Cody's dad got sick, and that Devon ever met his evil ex-boyfriend. "You did what you thought was right for you at the time."

"I let a broken heart chase me out of town. That was a stupid decision." Anger curls through his words and flashes through his features. "He wasn't worth it."

Surprise holds me still for a moment. Devon never talks about this. I hate that he has regrets. "I didn't know you felt that way."

His scrutiny shifts to members of The Fury, and then

flicks to Patrick and Cody. With a sigh, he collapses onto the barstool behind him. "Yeah, well I've been thinking about a lot since I turned thirty. I mean, I'm happy enough doing what I do, with my life the way it is. I love that we still exist as a band, even if we've been limited in what we can produce and when we can play together. But I can't help wondering about how things could have been. About what could've happened if I'd stayed in LA. If we all had."

"Me too." Studying him, I down another mouthful of beer. So many nights on this tour, I've looked at The Fury and wondered *if only* about my friends. "You could move back."

"We're not eighteen anymore." His tone is contemplative, and that wistfulness is so heavy it swamps me. "We're thirty. We have commitments and responsibilities."

If I can shift that regret into hope, I will. "So what? If you're still hungry for something, let's make it happen. Hell, we all need a shakeup. We can figure out a way to record more often, get more songs out faster. Play some gigs."

The beginning of a smile curves his lips and light shines in his brown eyes. "Yeah? You mean it?"

"I do. I promise. We'll talk to Cody and Patrick this weekend and make plans."

"Thanks, Craig." His throat works for a moment, then Devon puts his hand on my shoulder and gently squeezes. "I'll let you get back to Ty."

I catch hold of his arm before he can move away. "Dev, we'll make something good happen with the band."

"Playing together tomorrow for The Fury is a good start." Laughing, he rubs the back of his neck. "No pressure. Just playing for one of the biggest bands in rock."

"We're playing *with* them, man, not just for them. You're gonna blow them away."

He smiles at that. "Whatever happens, we're in it together."

We head back to the group. Brendan waves Devon over and Dev goes to him with a grin. Before my friends board their plane on Monday night, I'll make sure the four of us have a talk. If Devon's been upset, maybe Patrick and Cody have, too. I know I've been missing them. And this time on tour has shown me how much.

Ty stands from his perch on the chair, laughing with Cody, and turns his gaze my way. "I saw a lot of pictures. Your blond phase. The leather phase. The long hair phase. I liked them all."

Groaning, I wrap my arm around his waist. "The long hair phase wasn't my best look."

"I thought it was sexy." He leans in and kisses me and slides his hand through my hair. "Though, I love the way you look now."

The music throbbing from the speakers switches to a steady beat and I recognize the song as one I helped compose for Wild Intention, the first band Furious Records signed. To my left, Cody pulls Luke into matching his dance moves. I knew the pair would get along.

Ty tips his head, listening. "Hey, that song is on my Craig playlist."

Smiling, I set my beer on the table then slip my other arm around him. We sway, off beat, to the song. "I should start a Ty playlist. All the songs we dance to."

He brushes his hand along the back of my neck. "I remember the one we kissed to at the bar the day we met. I like the idea of a Craig and Ty, special moments playlist."

"So do I." Lowering my head, I meet his waiting lips. His taste has been imprinted on my brain, and having it again, I realize how much I've craved him.

Ty sighs and settles against me, his hand diving into my hair as the kiss goes deeper. His lips part and he whispers my name, continuing with the roll of his hips and graze of his torso against mine. My hands flex and roam his back, the ripple of his muscles as he moves reminds me of us together in the hotel room the night before he flew back to Buffalo.

I want him again. Now. Desperately. The month we've been apart has built up to a deluge of desire. Ty's close enough for me to touch. He's here, live, not stuck behind a video screen.

We've spent time with everyone and as much as I love them, I want to wrap myself around Ty and hide away from the world. No distractions, just him and me, exploring this connection. Being each other's sole focus.

I drag my mouth from his and lean back, tracing my finger along the edge of his lower lip. "Let's go back to my room."

His hand curls into my shirt, right over my heart. The banked heat in his eyes grows brighter as his gaze searches mine. "Yeah?"

"I need you."

Ty nods, smiles, and releases his hold on my shirt, only to trail his fingers down my stomach and then link our hands together. "Let's go."

I draw him toward the doors. Patrick looks up. So do Cody and Luke. I wave to them and point to the exit. The music's too loud for them to hear me, and if we go over to them, I'm afraid we'll get caught up in more conversations.

Patrick smirks and waves us off. The security guard opens the door for us, and Ty and I step through and into the quiet hallway.

He leans his head on my shoulder as we head to the elevator. "I'm glad we hung out with everyone, and I got to meet them. But I need you too."

I tap the button then slip my arm around his shoulders. "I'm sorry about springing everyone on you. I didn't know they were coming until they knocked on my door. You arrived about five minutes after them."

"It's nice that they surprised you." Ty traces his fingers along the rose tattoo on my forearm. The elevator doors open and we step inside the car.

I hit the button for my floor. "This is not the way I thought our weekend would go. I'll make it up to you."

He slides his hand along my jaw and steps closer so he's all I see. "It's fine. I got to meet the most important people in your life. That's big, and I'm happy it happened. You've met Slater and Noah, so you've met mine too."

Grasping his hips, I pull him against me. "You're amazing. Do you know that?"

"I feel that way, around you." His gaze turns shy and he ducks his face into my neck.

I stroke my hand over his back, struck by his sweetness. The car stops at my floor and the doors open.

Ty pulls away. There's a flush in his cheeks. We head down the hallway. He waits while I dig the keycard from my pocket then follows me into the room.

"Make yourself comfortable." After kicking off my sneakers, I set my wallet on my suitcase. Ty moves his bag so it's beside mine and toes off his sneakers. Those tiny superhero symbols cover his socks.

He dips his hands into his pockets and bites his lip. With his chin tipped toward his chest, he looks at me, and that muted heat in his gaze blazes brighter. "You do, you know."

"I do, what?"

"Make me comfortable." He steps closer, tracing his

fingers along my arms. "People underestimate how important that is. I can be myself with you. I'm safe with you. That's a huge thing to me."

"I understand what you mean. Not having to keep a guard up is freeing." I bend my head and he lifts his to meet me halfway, and we sink into the kiss. I can relax with him too, and don't have to worry about being something that I'm not.

My hands close over his shoulders and I sweep them up his neck, then down again, and keep going lower, dragging my fingers over that soft T-shirt until I reach the hem. He helps me draw it up his torso and over his head, and when I twist to toss it onto the other bed, the warmth of his fingers sliding under my shirt, teasing along my skin encourages me to hurry.

I get rid of my shirt, throwing it in the general direction of the other bed without looking. Ty stoops to mouth kisses along my chest, and his hands work to open my jeans.

Groaning, I grab his waist, then his hips, gliding my hands over his soft skin while his mouth sends my need for him soaring.

Desire pulses in my blood as my jeans loosen and he drags them down my legs. The sight of him on his knees before me is straight out of my fantasies. "Ty…"

Sitting on his heels, he gazes up at me and slides his hands up my calves and thighs. He licks his lips. "Can I taste you?"

"Oh, fuck." I fist my throbbing cock through my boxers. "Anything you want."

He kneels up and his fingertips hook into my waistband. Instead of lowering it, he leans in and rubs his cheek over me. Pre-cum spurts out, turning a patch of the cotton a darker shade of red. "I've thought about this. A lot."

I release my hold of myself in favor of sliding my fingers

through his hair. "I have too. You on your knees for me. You in so many ways. Just you."

Ty eases the boxers down, freeing my cock. He fists me with one hand while the other pushes the boxers to the pool of denim at my ankles. Those big brown eyes look up and meet mine, and he takes me into his mouth.

Wet heat. Soft tongue. Gentle suction. Individual sensations swamp me. On a moan, I adjust my stance and cup the back of his head. His other hand cradles my balls, while the hand on my cock works in tandem with his mouth, stroking me too close to the edge.

"Too close. Ty." Threading my fingers into his hair again, I ease him off me. "I'm not going to be able to last. Too excited you're here. I'll probably calm down after an orgasm, or five."

His smile is quick. "Good thing we have all night, then."

"Come here and kiss me." I extend my hand and he grabs hold, and I pull him to standing. Then I kick free of my pants and boxers, and ditch my socks.

Ty slides his hands up my chest and links them around my neck. His mouth lands on mine and his tongue traces the seam of my lips. I open for him, tangling our tongues together, and taking the kiss deeper.

I can't stop touching him, stroking his skin, addicted to the feel of his body pressed against mine. "One of us is wearing too many clothes."

His lips curve into a smile against mine. "Let me guess, it's me. Help me out with that?"

Dragging my knuckles down his chest and stomach, I wait for the catch in his breath and the way he sucks in and tightens his abs when I get close to his waistband. "Don't worry. I'll take care of you."

"I know you will." That trust in his eyes is damn addicting too.

I slide the button free of its hole, and the sound of his zipper lowering is music to my ears. His hands meet mine as we push the jeans down. I stoop to continue lowering them, and the superhero symbol covering the front of his boxers makes me pause. They're sexy and very Ty, and the star over his cock is like an X on a treasure map. "I like them."

"I'll get you a pair." He pushes into my hand as I stroke my fingers over the symbol. "They're, uh, comfortable. I… can't concentrate with you touching me like this."

I lift my hand. "Should I stop?"

He presses me against him. "No."

Smiling, I squeeze his cock. "You look good in them. But even better out of them."

Passion mists his eyes. "Then let's get me there."

His jeans are too tight to simply fall the rest of the way. I crouch and help him step out of them and take off his socks. Before I can reach for his boxers, he pushes them down. I grab the waistband and tug them free of his legs.

Stroking his cock, he backs up to the bed. "I have lube in my bag."

"I have it under my pillow."

He smirks. "Bet housekeeping got a kick out of that."

Laughing, I push him onto the mattress. "I put it there when I came in from the concert tonight."

"Oh." He glides his hand up my chest, hooks it behind my neck, then gently pulls me toward him. "For me? I mean, us?"

"Of course." I slide my hand under the pillow and snag the bottle. He takes it from me and presses the cap so it pops open. "What do you want tonight?"

"I want your hands on me. And I want you to kiss me.

And I want you inside me again." He drags his lower lip between his teeth. "But it's not just about me. What do you want?"

"You. Just you." I settle my weight on top of him. "Whether you're under me or over me. Whether it's my cock, fingers, or tongue inside you. Whether we do everything or nothing. I just want you." Then my cock rubs against his, and we both moan. "But I've been dreaming about being inside you since it happened. Felt like you were made for me."

Ty's fingers tremble on my shoulder. He gazes at me, and something Devon said a while ago about heart eyes pops into my head. I'm not sure if Ty has them. But I'm positive I do.

He leans in and kisses me. A slow press of lips, slip of tongue, and sigh that I feel deep in my soul. "Craig, I want everything with you."

"Then it's good we have all night. It just might take that long." I lean back on one arm and hold up my other hand for the lube.

Ty pours some into my palm, then his, and I set the bottle on the bedside table. His hand is on my cock before I can turn back to him. Groaning, I wrap my hand around his length and give him a slow slide inside my tight fist.

He arches into me and the hand he has on my thigh flexes over and over. "So good."

We drive each other higher and higher until the need to be inside him coils tighter and tighter and I'm about to break. I add more lube to my fingers and kiss him while I prep him, swallowing his gasps and moans and the whispered words of how he's ready to take me.

He puts the condom on me, gazing at me with expressive eyes, lips swollen from our kisses, and unsteady breaths.

I can't look away from his eyes as I slowly sink inside his tight heat. "You feel even better than I remembered. And what I remember was fucking incredible." My voice is raspy and low, all my concentration on not blowing my load as soon as I'm fully inside him.

His hands grasp my shoulder and thigh, like he wants to pull me onto him. His blunt nails dig into my skin. "Craig... The best..."

"Yeah, it is." I curl my hands under his shoulders and roll my hips, thrusting in and out, as my heart stutters and I know I'm on the edge of something big with Ty. Something life changing. Something that's been building since the moment we met and has no signs of stopping or slowing down.

Ty strokes himself, and on each thrust forward, his cockhead brushes my stomach. I speed up my thrusts, kiss him deeper, and with a long and broken moan, his release paints our skin.

His ass tightens around me, gripping me like a vise, and I'm gone, spurting inside him, grinding my hips against his ass to get as deep as I can. Pleasure is both sharp and soft rolling through me.

Panting, I drop onto him. His hands brush over my back and I listen to his heartbeat and breathing return to normal.

He kisses my temple and the top of my head. I need to get up so I don't crush him. I push onto my forearms and as soon as my mouth is near his, he kisses me.

My cock slips out of him. Grasping the condom, I shift onto my knees. "Be right back."

I deal with the condom, then clean up in the bathroom. Ty comes in and pulls me into the shower. We kiss again under the hot spray, soaping each other up, then dry each other off and slip back in bed.

We lay together, Ty in my arms. I gaze at him, wondering how I got so lucky. He's everything, talented, smart, funny, sexy, and sweet.

Holding him feels so good. So right. Like I'm right where I belong.

I wake to the scent of coffee and the feel of Ty next to me. Sunlight filters through the sheer white curtains, casting pale light over the room. Stroking my hand along his chest, I mouth a path of kisses from his shoulder to his neck, then cheek, then lips. What a great way to start the day. "Morning."

"Morning." Ty opens for me, taking the kiss a bit deeper, warm and soft and tasting of coffee and mint. "Want some coffee?"

"Please."

He sits up and shifts back to claim his mug from the bedside table then waits for me to adjust the pillows behind my back. The coffee is hot, sweet, and light. I down a few more sips, chasing away the cobwebs of sleep. "Have you been awake for long?"

"Long enough to make the coffee and check messages." The sheet pools at his waist. He holds up his phone, open to a string of texts. "Cody sent a lot of pictures. Looks like they had a great time hanging out with the band. He sent them to you too. Group text with *all* of us. Your friends, The Fury, you, and me."

"Yeah?" I grab my phone from the table on my side of the bed and open the message thread. "Want your coffee back?"

"Keep it. I'll make more." The mattress dips then rises as Ty rolls to his feet. He pads to the coffeemaker. His body is a work of art, all that soft skin and the angles and planes. I follow the lines of his body and the way the light plays over his form.

Want and need and an appreciation for all that he is floods through me. "If I could draw, I'd sketch you like that."

He twists towards me. "Fixing coffee naked?"

"I don't mean the coffee part. Just you, standing there, like you're an artist's muse, ready to be captured in a sculpture, painting, drawing, or photograph."

The coffee gurgles and hisses and the scent of freshly brewed beans fills the air. Ty smiles. "I'd pose for you. I want to sketch you too. You have no idea how good you look right now. Rumpled from sleep, all those muscles, that gorgeous face, with the blankets pooled around you. It's like an invitation to dive in and join you."

I angle my head to the spot he vacated. "You have an open invitation to join me in bed anytime you want."

The mug finishes filling with coffee. He snags one of the containers of creamer. "Did you see the texts yet?"

"No. I'll look now. Come back to bed. You're too far away." And I want to hold him.

A dozen messages from Cody show a photo timeline of last night's activities. One of him and Luke singing and dancing in the center of the lounge. Another of Landry and Patrick, labeled *twins*, due to their jackets and mirroring poses leaning against the bar. One of Devon and Luke on the couch, huddled close in conversation. Selfies of Cody with Zander and Brendan, then more of him with Devon and Patrick. A yearning ache to be there, sharing the experience with my friends, hits me in the chest.

Ty returns with a steaming mug. Biting his lip, he climbs onto the bed. "I'm sorry you missed out on spending time with them." Voice soft, he inches his hand onto my thigh, as though he's unsure of his welcome. "We should've stayed with everyone."

"No." No way will I let him walk on eggshells, worried

that I'll resent him for this. I rush to set the coffee mug and phone on the table then turn toward him and frame my hand along the side of his face. "I'm not sorry about stealing you away so we could be together. I wouldn't trade my time with you for anything."

The lines of uncertainty smooth and he curls into my side. "I wouldn't trade my time with you either. But—"

"But nothing." His hair is soft. I love sliding my fingers through it as I cup the back of his head. "You're here. *Here*. With me. When I didn't think I'd get to see you for weeks. Do you know how happy that makes me?"

His brows lift and hope fills his eyes. "Very?"

Nodding, I lean in and brush my lips across his. "Ecstatic."

Light returns to his gaze and his smile warms his features like a sunbeam. He sets his coffee aside, then wraps his arms around me. "Me too."

Holding him close, I settle against the pillows. "What's our plan for today? We have to check out of the room by eleven, but we don't have to be at Luke's until four. There's a cafe nearby. We can get breakfast there. Then drop our stuff at my place. After that, we'll figure out what's next." I want to experience everything with him, but would also be content lazing about and doing nothing together. The together part is all that matters.

"Can we go to that coffee shop again? And maybe you could give me another piano lesson?" His gaze dips to my mouth, then those light brown eyes burn with an intensity that takes my breath away. "I don't care what we do, Craig. I just want to be with you."

This man is going to wreck me.

Music twists and pulses through Luke's home studio. I play the chords, with Brendan on drums, Patrick on bass, Cody and Luke singing into a mic together, then Zander joins in, harmonizing with them. They sound good, really good. And Cody has the theatrics that make him a great frontman. Just like Luke.

We've been at it for close to two hours. All of us who can play multiple instruments have taken a turn on just about everything. We've played in duos, trios, quads, and singles in the case of Devon's drum solo, and in combinations of our own band members, and mixing them up too. Even Ty played the drums under Brendan and Devon's tutelage.

Ty meets my gaze and my skin prickles with awareness, whether he's watching me or he's laughing and talking with my friends, there's a connection threading us together. The way he felt under me last night, and how he and I touched as much as we could throughout the hours we claimed for ourselves this morning and afternoon has strengthened it so much, I wouldn't be surprised to see a current of energy connecting us to each other. He lights me up, like he's flicked a switch and everything is brighter and better. I wish he didn't have to go home tomorrow.

The song draws to a close. Ty and Landry applaud us, then Cody turns to Luke and gives him a winning smile. "I thought you and Paddy were going to sing for us."

With his arm around Cody, Luke swings them to face Patrick. "You up for it, Patrick? We did say we'd do it."

He rolls his eyes, but he's smiling. "Fine." With quick movements, he slips his bass off and places it in his guitar case.

"Yes!" Cody punches the air. "You guys need anything, like groupies holding up their phones with the flashlights on and swaying to the music? I can do that for you."

Barking a laugh, Zander rolls his shoulder and flexes the arm he'd broken. Today, he was finally able to play without pain. He waves Cody to his side. "I like this one. He's fun."

"Fun. Right." Patrick's tone is as dry as dust. He drags a stool forward and accepts the acoustic guitar Luke hands him.

He strums it as Luke settles onto a stool too, then plays the opening chords. I remember this song, and this period of time in a tumultuous few years of disastrous bands filled with drama that Patrick endured.

Luke starts off singing. There isn't much he can't do vocals-wise, and this song is right in the middle of his range. Then Patrick takes the next verse. His voice has a bite to it, a snarl that grabs the listener by the throat. It's a sucker punch, and it's awesome.

I look at Devon, Ty, Zander, Landry, Brendan, and Cody. They're all riveted. When the song ends, silence reigns for a good ten seconds before everyone bursts out with how much they loved it.

Luke claps Patrick on the shoulder. "This guy owns the rights, so we could do something with it."

The right side of Patrick's mouth lifts in a partial smile. "You want to record it? It's a good song, but I only want to do it with you."

"We'll talk." Luke gets off the stool and drags it to the side of the room. "I'd love for you and your bandmates to do a song for us."

Brendan welcomes Devon to his drum kit, handing over the sticks with a flourish. Patrick straps on his bass again. Luke waves Cody over to his mic. My friends get situated, chatting and joking with the band. And I stay where I am, guitar at the ready, saturated in the surreal feeling of being in this space with my friends.

Ty stands beside Zander, but his smile is all for me.

One hand on the mic stand, Cody turns to me. "What song should we do?"

"Better Days Ahead?" The song, the last one we recorded back in December, is the first that comes to mind. I play the opening chord.

Patrick joins in, then Devon, and it's like no time has passed at all. Cody's voice caresses the lyrics, and I can't stop the smile from overtaking my face. This is perfect.

To my left, Brendan and Landry stand with Ty, Zander, and Luke. Having The Fury watch us play gives me a rush, a twisting mix of nerves and pride. My best friends are here with me and no matter what happens or what anyone thinks of our sound, nothing can take away sharing this experience.

Beside me, Cody sways as he sings and gives me a thumb's up when I add my voice to the chorus. Devon, at home behind the drum kit, nods his head along with the beat he taps out. Keeping in sync with Devon, Patrick wanders closer to him, and the two grin at each other.

The song flows seamlessly, as if we just performed it yesterday instead of months ago. Between Cody's confident command of the words, and Devon, Patrick, and I nailing the notes and rhythm, no one misses a beat.

We come to the song's end, with Cody's voice hanging in the air for the final note, unadorned with instruments. He dips his head in a dramatic pose, holding the mic stand like he would a lover. Then he pops back up, and grins.

The Fury and Ty break into applause, and Landry whistles. Ty beams at us. "That. Was. Awesome."

"Great sound, Cody." Brendan salutes him with a mini-pack of gummy bears, his trademark treat. "Nice job on bass, Patrick. Devon, you killed it, too. Let's hear it for the rhythm section."

"Thanks, Bren." Patrick reaches over the drum kit to high-five Devon.

"You're as good as always, man." Brendan tosses me one of his mini-packs. I set it beside my guitar case.

When I turn back, he is on the opposite side of the room, joining his bandmates in a huddle. My throat thickening, I glance from Patrick to Cody to Devon. "This really was something."

Cody sets the mic on the stand. "It was everything. Damn, I've missed us."

Devon catches my gaze. Taking a deep breath, he brushes his hand through his hair. "I have, too. Craig and I were talking last night. I'd like us, as a band, to do more, if we can."

Patrick's eyes narrow in concern and he wanders close to the drum kit again before throwing a questioning look my way. "Sure, Dev, whatever you need."

Off to the side, Luke, Zander, Brendan, and Landry are still huddled together in a whispered conversation, one that's causing Ty's eyes to grow wide. His gaze flicks to mine and he mouths, *Wow*.

The quad separates then joins us. Luke claims the space close to the mic, his natural place. "Honestly, you blew us away."

Pride puffs me up. The guys and I exchange grins. "Thanks, bud."

Zander stands shoulder to shoulder with him. "So much that we'd like to sign your band to our label."

Surprise keeps me frozen in place. I'm sure my expression mirrors the shock on my friends' faces. Cody gasps. "You want to sign us?"

Luke and Brendan nod, while Zander and Landry both open their mouths and start talking at the same time.

They stop, laugh, and Zander gestures for Landry to go ahead.

"We enjoyed the hell out of spending time with you guys last night, watching you all interact then and today. Listening to you play together, we know you have something special," Landry says.

"Devon and I talked last night about music and performing and what went down when he and Cody left LA." With a gentle squeeze to Cody's shoulder, Luke sends him then Devon a sympathetic smile. "It was a good talk."

Devon glances at me. Guilt stamps his features and his shoulders curl him inward. "I wasn't trying to go over anyone. Luke's a good listener."

I wave away his worry as I set my guitar in its case. "I'm not angry. We were going to talk to Cody and Patrick this weekend anyway."

"You were? About what?" Hugging himself, Cody inches toward Patrick, and Patrick shifts his bass aside and wraps a protective arm around Cody's shoulders.

"About what I said a minute ago, how I want us to do more. I need it." Color staining his cheeks, Devon stammers and steps out from behind the drum kit. "I'd love for the four of us to have a real shot at making something. But I was afraid it was too late, that we blew our chance."

Luke flicks a guitar pick between his fingers in a move that I've seen him do often enough to know half the time he doesn't realize he's doing it. "I don't believe in too late, or only having one chance. Do you know how many chances we've had?" He gestures to his bandmates. "Hell, these guys alone have given me several. If you have supportive people by your side, you can do anything."

Zander's hand comes down on Luke's shoulder. Their friendship has made headlines. Through thick and thin, they've been there for each other. "With us behind you, you'd have all the support and resources you'd need."

Hope twists through my chest. "You're really serious about this?"

"We never joke about business." Luke tosses the guitar pick to me. "We like your sound and your vibe. I think you'd be a good fit with our label. These guys agree." He jerks his thumb toward his bandmates. "Craig and Patrick, you've always been there for us. We'd do anything we could to help you guys. My talk with Devon last night got me thinking, and watching you play together today cemented the idea. I've already thought of a few bands you could open for. Get you touring. Get you in the studio. Get Falling Midnight's music to the masses."

Energy tingles under my skin. After Cody and Devon moved away from LA, I thought we'd never have a chance to share a stage again. Having the opportunity now is unreal. I move closer to my friends. "Doing this with you guys would be a dream come true for me. I want this."

Devon clutches my arm, the wistfulness in his features pulling at my heart. "So do I."

Cody pumps his arm in the air. "Hell, yeah. Let's do it."

Features etched in indecision, Patrick white-knuckles the guitar's strap, gripping it like a shield, his gaze lingering on Cody before landing on the framed photo of The Fury on stage in front of a massive arena filled with fans. "I... don't know."

"Come on, Paddy." Cody's expressive eyes are wide and pleading. Gripping his hands together over his heart, he leans into Patrick. "I always wondered what would've happened if my dad hadn't gotten sick, and I could've stayed in LA with you guys. Doing this would mean a lot to me. Please."

Looking at Cody, Patrick seems to search for something. I

hold my breath as their silent conversation continues for the longest minute of my life. Finally, Patrick's hesitation gives way to a nod. "Okay. I'm in."

"Thank you!" Cody throws his arms around Patrick and plants a loud peck on his cheek. Then he spins away and hugs Luke, Zander, then Brendan and Landry. "Thank you so much for the opportunity."

Chuckling, Luke claps him on the back. "No problem. Together, we'll take Falling Midnight to the next level."

Zander extends his hand toward mine, enveloping me in a warm shake. "Welcome to the Furious Records family. We'll have a contract sent over. Take your time and have your people look over it, and then we can all sit down together."

"This is incredible. Thank you." I follow up the handshake with a hug. "This means a lot to me."

"Well, you mean a lot to us." He steps back and gets enveloped in a hug from Devon. Our friend may be small, but he's all wiry strength and manages to knock Zander back a step.

I know how careful they are with their label. Furious Records is everything to these men. There's no way they'd offer us a contract if they didn't believe we could give them something special. I shake hands with Luke. "We won't let you down."

"I know you won't." He claps me on the shoulder. "Satyr's Kiss has an East Coast tour coming up in the fall. You could open for them, go on after the local band, do a five song set."

Energy tingles through me. "That would be amazing."

"Good. I'm so freaking happy you're one of us now." Luke hugs me again. Then he pulls Patrick in for a longer one. They're laughing and murmuring, and I feel like a weight's been lifted off my shoulders. The four of us will need to have a serious talk about what happens with Cody and Devon's jobs if we're touring and then for recording too. Patrick and I have the most flexibility there.

Devon turns away from Zander, and bangs into Luke. They hug, and then Devon comes to me, rubbing his hand over the back of his neck, surprise still tinging his features. "I can't believe this is happening."

"It's surreal." I wrap my arm around his neck and tug him closer, using him as an anchor because I feel so fucking high, there has to be at least three feet of air between my feet and the floor. "It's good. Really good. Dev, I'm not stopping until we're at the top of the charts."

His smile is the one I remember he wore the day we all decided to move to LA together. He mirrors my move and the weight of his arm lands on my shoulders, grounding me. "I'm not blowing this shot. Nothing's gonna get in my way this time. I know we need to figure out the details, but I'll do whatever it takes."

Brendan slings his arm over Devon's shoulders, and I drop my arm. "Come on, bud. We have so much to talk about." They wander away, with Brendan giving him a rundown of the other bands under the Furious Records label.

Ty weaves past them, heading for me. His vibrant pink *Supervillains are Heroes Too* shirt almost glows under the lights. He throws his arms around me, enveloping me in his exuberance. "Congratulations! This is so cool. And you said you weren't a rockstar."

Cody bounds over and wraps his arms around us. The energy pouring off him is intense. "Falling Midnight is back, baby! Maybe Ty can tweak our band's logo?"

"We could use an update." As exciting as the prospect of working with my best friends is, I want to share this moment with Ty and Ty alone. But with Cody wrapped around us like a python, I can't move. So, the best I can do is kiss the tip of Ty's nose.

Ty squeezes me tighter. His gorgeous lips spread wide and his eyes sparkle with as much enthusiasm as when he talks about new story ideas for his comic. "I'd be happy to create something for you."

"Come on, everyone," Luke calls. "Time for food. Let's head up to the deck."

"I'm starving." After giving us one more squeeze, Cody spins away and makes a beeline for Luke.

Devon and Brendan are deep in discussion by the drum kit, and Cody has claimed both Zander and Luke's attention as the trio walk toward the stairs. I catch Patrick watching them go, his expression unreadable, before Landry claps him on the back and says something that makes him laugh.

Ty drops his arms from around my neck, but catches my hand and laces our fingers together. "You looked so happy playing with your band."

I run the pad of my thumb over his knuckle. "Playing with the guys feels better, more right, than anything else I've been a part of. There's something about them. It's... the way things are supposed to be."

"Luke and the guys were right. There's something special when the four of you play together. The energy, the connectedness..." He shakes his head. "I can't explain it, but it's extraordinary."

We watch the others troop up the stairs. I release Ty's hand to tuck the pack of gummy bears into his bag, in front of his sketchbook. "When Cody moved back to Buffalo, we tried finding a replacement for him, but no one was right. Probably, because no one was him. When Devon left, we didn't even try because we knew no one could measure up, so we put the band on hiatus. Once things settled down for Cody's dad, I began sending the guys snippets of lyrics that came to me. We all worked on the music. The occasional recordings kept us connected, but I didn't think much more could happen. Now, we have a chance for so much more. And being backed by people I trust is huge."

Ty holds out his hand for me to take, then laces our fingers together again, like it's the most natural thing in the world. "Cody's so excited. Devon too. Patrick's harder for me to read."

"Patrick's... Well, he's Patrick. If he didn't want to do it, he'd say so." I lead him up the stairs. The sliding glass doors to the deck are open and a salty sea breeze blows over us. The others are in the kitchen, so we have the stretch of wooden beams dotted with potted palm trees overlooking the ocean to ourselves. "He and Cody fight over stupid things enough now as it is. I can't imagine how it'll be if we're all sharing a tour bus on the road."

"Maybe things will be different this time. You're all older." Ty slips his arm through mine, as if he can read my mind and knows I want him closer.

I bump my shoulder into his, and grin. "You saw them in the hotel room. I doubt it."

Ty's gaze shifts to my friends in question. "There's an energy between those two. I'm surprised the air itself doesn't ignite."

"That's always been there." I follow his gaze to where Patrick's eyes keep flicking to Cody every time Cody laughs. "It comes out a lot more when they're around each other in person, than say, a video call. Over the last several years, the four of us have only been together for a handful of days at a time, so I don't know what will happen when we are around each other a lot more, or if it'll be the same as it was when we lived together ten years ago. I guess we'll find out."

He rests his chin on my shoulder, his grin intoxicating. "It's exciting though, isn't it? Another chance at your dream?"

"It really is."

"I can't believe I got to see The Fury offer you guys a contract. I'm so happy for you." He unwraps himself from me, and I miss the feel of his body molded to mine. But when he holds out his hand and says, "Hi. I'm Falling Midnight's biggest fan," my laughter barks out.

He's too sweet. "I'll take you up on your super fan status."

"Hats, shirts, whatever merch you have, I'll wear it proudly."

"It takes a super fan to know a super fan. Get me something with your hockey player superhero on it. No wait, give me the supervillain."

Ty's eyes widen. "You'd really wear my villain?"

"Of course. Like your shirt says," I trace my finger over the script on his chest, "Supervillains are heroes too."

He links his arms around my neck, his tawny eyes shining, and the softest of smiles on his lips. "I really want to kiss you."

I glide my hands along his ribcage, up and down, back and forth, to get a feel for him, and bend my head to meet his waiting lips. They're soft and open on his quiet pant. Angling my head, I take the kiss deeper, delving into his warm, wet heat. He kisses like a dream, giving me all of himself, and I do the same.

Leaning into me, he looks out at the ocean. "I could get used to this view. It's soothing."

"You're welcome to visit me anytime. I don't have an ocean view, but it's not too far to find one." I tip his face to mine, wanting to give him everything. "What do you say about spending tomorrow at the beach? We have a lot of time before you have to be at the airport."

He buries his face in my chest. "I don't want to think about leaving."

"Neither do I." Wrapping my arms around him, I hold him close, breathing in his scent. Parting tomorrow isn't going to be any easier than saying goodbye to him last time. If anything, it'll be harder.

His book launch party is in three weeks. I'm already counting down the days until we can see each other again.

CHAPTER NINE
TY

Entering the art gallery that Noah chose as the venue for our comic book's launch party, I am more than ready for a cocktail. Our book's release day has been more stressful than I anticipated. From dealing with my roommate removing my wet clothes from the dryer mid-cycle because he deemed drying his clothes to be more important than mine, to customers yelling at me over issues with claims that are out of my control at work, to responding to the hundreds of comments on our social media posts for the book, it's been a very long day.

Behind me, Slater and Noah jostle each other, rushing inside to avoid the rain that's increased to a steady drizzle. Slater pulls the door shut behind us. "It would be cool if we could control the weather. Our next superhero or villain needs to be able to do that."

"Good idea." I wish I had superpowers of my own. Ones that could get me across the rainy city without the need to drive, or compel my roommate to not eat food labeled with my name, or teleport me to Craig anytime I want.

The soles of my red high tops squeak on the polished

floor. My black tee and dark jeans aren't what I'd planned to wear tonight, thanks to the drama with the dryer, but Craig's leather jacket gives the outfit an edge. He lent it to me when I was in LA, in case I got cold during the flight home. It smells like him, and the scent calms me.

Colorful posters featuring the characters in our series dominate the walls of the art gallery. Panel after panel, like something I'd see at a comic book convention. But this is *our* work, *our* characters, and it's amazing. Mouth agape, at a loss for words, I turn to Slater. He looks as surprised as I feel.

Behind him, Noah steps up, grinning, and lays his hands on our shoulders. "Congratulations. I'm so proud of you both."

Swallowing hard, I find my voice. "Noah... This is amazing. Thank you."

A large table holds stacks of paperback copies of our book. Another table has a tiered cake in the colors of our hero and villain. Themed treats and signature cocktails decorate a third table. The tablecloths are the same blue as our superhero's hockey uniform, and the cocktail napkins are imprinted with both the hero and villain's likenesses. Noah has outdone himself.

Slater grabs him and pulls him into a tight hug. The emotion working over my ginger friend's face tugs at my heart. As a kid, Slater had trouble reading, and his mother getting him into comic books encouraged a love he might never have found otherwise. He still has reading difficulties now, and told me early on in our working together that he hoped our books would help people like him to not give up either.

Leaning back, he brushes his hand along Noah's face. "I can't believe you did all this. Thank you."

Noah clasps his wrist, holding him in place. "Anything for you. I love you."

"I love you too." He bends his head, drawing Noah closer, into a kiss.

Smiling at the pair, I step around them and take a video panning the room. I want to remember everything about tonight.

We've put in countless hours on the project. Early feedback for the comic is positive. My phone has been going off all day with notifications. Pride at what Slater and I have accomplished together fills me. Collaborating with him on this feeds so many parts of my soul.

A bunch of Slater and Noah's Buffalo Bedlam teammates, other friends, and a few of my co-workers mill around the bright, modern space, drinking cocktails, taking in the comic book artwork, and talking. I'm swept up in a sea of hugs, handshakes, and well wishes.

I should be happy. And I am. But I miss Craig.

He is supposed to be here, but instead of arriving yesterday, work kept him in LA an extra day. He texted me from the airport a while ago, but traffic is a mess, the rain isn't helping things, and I don't know when he'll arrive.

I end the video, then take a few photos. No new text updates appear from Craig.

It's been three weeks since our weekend together in LA. He's been busy with collaboration meetings with clients, songwriting for his own band, and duties for the foundation. He and his friends signed the contract with Furious Records, then did an impromptu studio session, playing *Better Days Ahead* the same day Craig recorded the duet with Luke. After the Fury released the song on their social media channels, the video went viral, and Falling Midnight's star has been steadily rising.

I can't help but worry over what will happen when the band dominates his time. Things are already changing. He's pulled in so many directions. Will he grow too busy to want to keep talking to some guy on the other side of the country?

I'm terrified the answer to that could be yes.

Slater gently nudges my shoulder. "What's wrong? You look worried."

Blinking at him, I paste on a smile. "No, I'm good."

Noah crosses his arms over his chest. "Want to try that again? Talk to us."

My face heating, I gesture to the crowded room. "We have guests."

"Who are all enjoying themselves. We can take a few minutes. Talk."

I tuck my phone into my pocket. "Fine. Craig's on his way here to support me tonight, but aside from that, we've only spent two weekends together in person. I feel so connected to him, but I've been thinking about what happens to our relationship now that his band has plans for recording and touring. Will he get too busy for me?"

Slater's expression turns doubtful. "Every time I turn around, you guys are texting each other. Like the other night, when you were so distracted with those texts, Noah said it reminded him of how I used to be."

I snort. "Yeah, right. I am nowhere near your level of social media addict. Though, you have gotten a lot better."

"Your phone is in your hand as often, if not more than, Slater's." Noah lifts his chin and his expression dares me to argue. Which I can't, as Noah is correct about the amount of times I look at my phone.

"I can't help it. Talking to Craig is one of my favorite things. I always want more. And I never know when something will come in, so I check it a lot. His hours are getting odder and he's so busy now, I don't hear from him as often as before."

I open my phone's photo gallery and angle the screen so the guys can see it. "He sent me flowers today for the book release." Red roses, yellow sunflowers, and blue delphinium. They're the same colors as the book cover's graphics. And that superhero congratulations card continues the theme.

Leaning into Slater, Noah smiles at me. "He put a lot of care into this."

"I know. It made my day. There was a small box of chocolate truffles too that also matched the book cover. My pain in the ass roommate swiped the box and ate them."

Slater exchanges a look with Noah, and they both turn toward me, side by side, like a united front. "You should just move in with us."

"What? Are you serious?"

"You should," Noah agrees. "But we can talk about that later. Back to Craig, if he didn't care, why would he send the gift that he clearly put time and thought into, and why would he come tonight?"

Dragging my hand through my hair, I huff out a breath and then roll my shoulders to dislodge the frenzied uncertainty residing there. "I don't know. I'm just... scared. We've never had the conversation about labeling what this is. Maybe things would be different if we lived closer together, but I feel like the distance and time difference are making things more complicated. I know what I want..."

"And what's that?" Noah's question is simple. Only three words. But they are asking me to spill the longings of my soul.

"Him." I can't leave it at that, because even though the answer is true, it's entirely too vague. "I want what you guys have—with him."

Slater raises a brow. With his towering height, arms crossed over his wide chest, and no-nonsense expression, he looks every bit the enforcer, the protector he is on the ice for his hockey team. "You need to have that conversation with him."

"I know..." Plucking at my shirt cuff, I give voice to my fears. "What if he doesn't want what I want?"

Noah's features crease in sympathy. He shifts closer and lays his hand on my shoulder. "Then that would suck, but at least you'd know. And there's always the other, happier scenario: What if he wants the same thing as you? You're eventually giving your hero and villain a happily ever after, right? So why shouldn't you have one?"

"Exactly," Slater adds. "You're our friend and we want you to be happy. And Craig makes you happy. So talk to him."

My gaze bounces between the two men and my thoughts spin. For my own peace of mind, I need to do it, no matter how vulnerable I feel. Excitement and nerves whirl like mini tornadoes in my gut.

In a year of change, it is time to take another leap. And if I crash and burn, my friends will be there to help me through it.

As if Slater is reading my mind, he lays his hand on my shoulder. "No matter what happens, we're here for you."

"Thank you." Gratitude for the two men wells deep, washing away some of my nerves. "You'd really let me move in with you?"

"You should. With how often you've been over, it's like you're living there anyway. You don't need the stress of inconsiderate people making your life more difficult." Noah nods his thanks to one of the servers and takes the plate she hands him filled with snacks. "Plus, we like having you around."

After years of feeling like a burden when I was growing up, hearing that I am wanted and liked squeezes something in my chest. "I'd like that."

"Good. We'll do the official thing of adding you with the management company later this week." Slater snags two cookies from the plate and hands me one. "If you and Craig want to stay over tonight, you can. Then you won't have to deal with your roommates."

"He's staying with Devon for this visit. But he was going to stay with me tonight. We'll take you up on that." More people have arrived, and Craig and Patrick aren't with them. I need something to calm my nerves. "If you guys don't mind, I think I'll head over to try one of the cocktails."

"Go ahead. We'll catch up with you in a bit."

Various Bedlam players join me on the way to the bar. They suggest the comic book for our next book club pick. I'm touched by their support and I also have to laugh because Noah, who has next month's pick, told Slater and me today that he's choosing it for sure. I choose the drink named for our villain. It has whiskey, champagne, honey, and a squeeze of lemon juice. The cocktail is strong, and I take small sips as I chat with the guys.

A few of us drift away to the food, and I take a photo of that too. I'm starving, and stuff a sugar cookie decorated like our superhero's mask into my mouth. The crowd shifts, giving me a view of the front doors. One opens, and Devon and Cody enter the building. I wash down the cookie with the rest of my drink and wave my hand high, catching their attention.

"Ty!" Cody's exuberant voice hits me seconds before his hug engulfs me in a tight embrace. There are raindrops glistening in his dark hair, and scattered drops dot the shoulders and arms of his pink button-down. Beaming, he pulls back and his glance bounces around the room before returning to mine. His eyebrow piercing glints in the light. "Congratulations. Great party."

"Thanks for coming. The party is all due to Noah." I point to where Noah and Slater are standing across the room. "Slater's the redhead who co-wrote the series with me. Noah's the dark-haired one beside him. He's Slater's boyfriend and the one who put the party together."

"Oh, I know who they are. I've seen Bedlam games with Devon." He gives a sly smile to Devon, who is standing next to him.

Clad in a blazer, T-shirt, and jeans, Devon tears his gaze from a group of Bedlam players. Clasping my hand, he pulls me in for a quick hug. "Congratulations on the series. I bought my copy this morning."

"Thank you." They were so nice to me that weekend in LA, making me feel included right away, and they've kept it up since, whether we're texting in the group chat about the logo I tweaked for them, or about whatever randomness they come across in their daily lives. "How are you guys doing? It seems like your *Better Days Ahead* video is everywhere."

"Right? It's wild." Cody practically vibrates, and it's clear his excitement from The Fury's offer to now has not dissipated in the slightest. "When we were hanging out in the studio to support Craig, and Luke asked us if we wanted to play together like we did at his place, I couldn't begin to imagine the reaction we've received. It's unreal."

"It really is." Devon's voice is soft, threaded with wonder as though he still can't believe the positive response. "We're seeing a lot of downloads of our other songs too. I'm really happy we had you make our logo better. It's badass now. I'm proud of people seeing it."

Pride pushes me to stand taller. I'd sent ideas for tweaks to the four of them and incorporated everyone's input. "Glad you like it."

"Luke and the rest of The Fury do too." Devon peers at the pictures lining the wall, open admiration in his gaze. "You should do the artwork for our album. You're amazing."

Working with them was interesting and entertaining, and I'd do it again in a heartbeat. "I'd be honored."

He nods, like that's settled. "Craig texted me, saying that he should be here soon. He and Patrick hit heavy traffic on the way from the airport."

"He texted me too. I hope it clears up soon."

Cody grabs my arm and points across the room to where a group of the hockey players have congregated near the bar. "I didn't know your Bedlam buddies were coming. Is the *entire* hockey team here? Celek looks good in that shade of blue."

Devon's head whips in that direction. "*Celek's* here?"

What Cody said about Devon's interest in the team captain when we were in LA flashes into my mind. Maybe I should attempt to play Cupid. Cody would. And if I don't, I'm sure he will. "The team came to support Slater, and me too, well, the ones that know me anyway. These guys always show up for each other." I wrap my arm around Devon's biceps. "Come meet Celek."

His eyes widen and he stiffens as though he's frozen to his spot. "Really?"

"Sure. Unless you don't want to?"

"No, I do." He sucks in a breath and smooths a hand over his chest. His pupils are blown wide. "I'm just nervous."

Cody steps in and fixes Devon's hair. "You look great. You're *amazing*. He's the lucky one, getting to meet you."

That makes Devon crack a smile. "Thanks for being my hype man."

I remember how nervous I'd been walking to Craig's booth the day after we'd met. "Celek's really nice. He'll like that you do the book club with us."

He sucks in a breath, then exhales in a rush. "Okay. Yeah. Let's do this."

"You coming, Cody?" I don't want anyone feeling left out.

"I'll wait here. Dev, you'll be fine." He stares into Devon's eyes like he can make his statement true through sheer willpower. "I'll do a walk by in a few minutes. If you need me, I'll swoop in."

"Thanks," Devon says.

With a tug on Devon's jacket cuff, I lead him a step forward. Then, we're side by side, and weaving through the partygoers.

Celek looks up as we approach. He smiles at me, and then his gaze moves to Devon. His brows lift and interest flares in his brown eyes. He extends his hand, his smile deepening. "I don't believe we've met."

Devon's breath trembles as his and Celek's hands lock in an embrace. "Devon Milne. I'm a friend of Ty's."

"Anton Celek. Everyone calls me Celek." Celek shifts closer, still holding his hand. "It's good to meet you, Devon."

"You too. I'm a big fan." Devon's throat bobs and he licks his lips like he's gone days without water. "Of the team, I mean. But you're my favorite player." His voice pitches high. He closes his eyes, clears his throat, then opens them. "I loved your last pick for the book club."

"The mystery? Yeah, that was a good one. Did you know a sequel is coming out next month?"

"I pre-ordered it. I'm looking forward to seeing what they throw at the detective next. The premise sounds really good."

"Oh, I have *thoughts* on that..." Celek moves his hand to Devon's elbow. "Can I get you a drink?"

They only have eyes for each other, so my work here is done. I take a step back, catch Cody watching us from across the room, and grin as he gives me a thumbs up.

"Ty!" Slater waves me toward him. "Can we get a quick photo? I just realized we didn't take one together yet, and don't want to miss out on doing it."

"Oh, sure." I glance around us. "Let's stand in front of the poster of the book cover."

He snags a copy of the paperback for us to hold too. "Dream come true, bud. Thanks for making it happen with me."

We pose, our arms around each other, as Noah, with his phone in hand, lines us up in his shot. "We make a good team. I can't wait to get started on the next one."

Noah takes a few photos, then at Slater's insistence, joins us, and hands his phone to someone else so they can play photographer.

After we finish with the photos, I walk through the room with my friends, sipping another villain's cocktail, and contemplating food. Two small cookies weren't enough. Devon is still talking to Celek, and a few other Bedlam teammates who are also in the book club have joined them. Cody's standing near Devon and holds the attention of two players who joined the team last season. The pair aren't in the book club, so I haven't met them yet.

The sound of the gallery's doors opening behind us brings in the patter of rain and swish of cars traveling on wet roads along with two low voices. I turn. Craig comes in, followed by Patrick. Brushing at the raindrops in his hair, he stops short and a smile bursts onto his face when his gaze meets mine. "Hey."

"You're here." Happiness surges through me like an electric charge. I put my glass on the nearest table then leap forward, wrapping my arms around Craig's firm torso, and tuck my head into the cradle of warm skin at his neck and shoulder. The familiar hint of cinnamon fills my senses and flashes me back to the first time I'd held him in an embrace.

Craig's arms band around me, locking us together. Soft lips graze my temple. "Feels good to hold you again."

That deep, husky voice and the breath feathering against my skin makes me shiver. I tighten my embrace and absorb the fiercely spoken words. "You too. I missed you."

"I got here as fast as I could. Congratulations on your book release. I'm so proud of you." One hand briefly leaves my back and Craig's head leans away for a moment. "Hello, Slater and Noah. Congratulations on the book, Slater."

"Hey, Craig." Noah's greeting is quickly followed by Slater's, "Thanks. Good to see you, man."

Beside us, Slater, Noah, and Patrick exchange hellos and introductions.

I know I should step back, but I can't let go of Craig, and his arms are still wrapped tight around me. The threat of tears burns behind my eyes. I bite my lip until the sensation passes. It's been such a stressful few weeks. I needed this so much. Needed him. Under control again, I raise my head and force myself to shift to his side, but we keep our arms around each other. "How was your flight?"

"Slow. And traffic was a mess. But I'm here, finally."

"Thank you for coming."

His soft smile is as gentle as the stroke of his finger along my cheek, and then the press of his lips against mine. "I wouldn't miss this."

My heart stumbles at the care in the gestures and the certainty in his words. They give me hope that he might want the same thing as me regarding the future of our relationship.

I catch Patrick's gaze. "Thanks for coming."

He leans in for a quick hug. "Congratulations on the release." His gaze scans the room, taking in the happy atmosphere. "Tonight, we can eat, drink, and be merry. Tomorrow, we get down to business. We've blocked out the next two weeks for writing the rest of the songs for the album, but we might not need all that time."

"Words are flowing for me." Craig slips his hand beneath my jacket and draws circles over my back. "We also have a good amount of material we've wanted to use for a while that's working well with the sound we're going for on this record."

I lean into his touch, studying the faint shadows beneath his eyes. "That's great. Maybe you'll have some downtime and can relax."

"I hope so. I want to spend time with you." His gaze drops to my chest and he smiles. "My jacket looks good on you."

"I like that it's yours." In his black button-down with the sleeves rolled to the elbows, and his legs encased in dark jeans, he is my tall, dark, and handsome superhero. I catch hold of his hand. "Can I get you a drink?"

"I wouldn't say no to that. But first, can you give me a closer look at the artwork on the walls?"

We walk to the posters. Craig stops by one of the villain and hero, locked in battle. "I'm really proud of you, Ty. You created this entire world, drew it out, formed the characters, gave them personalities, conflicts, and feelings. You're incredible."

It's not the first time Craig has admired my work. And just as it did when I saw my sketch of him hanging on his refrigerator, the flutter in my chest makes me lightheaded in the best possible way. "Slater and I worked hard. I never imagined his initial idea would springboard us into ideas for multiple stories, but it did. Sharing this with him is special."

"That's how I feel when I collaborate on a song with someone." He tucks me closer to his side as we pass a small crowd of people Slater and I know from the comic book store. We move on to another poster, showing the hero surrounded by his hockey team. "Did Slater put his teammates in the story?"

Laughing, I glance at the gaggle of Bedlam players. "Not intentionally. Though they all want to be included. You wouldn't believe the number of times they've asked. We're trying to figure out how to do it. I thought we might draw something special for the holidays and it can be our gift to the team."

He glances at the table loaded with the paperbacks. "I want to buy copies of the books to give to the older kids at the hospital. If you have extras left over after tonight, I'll take them. Otherwise, I can order some."

"You don't have to buy those. We'll donate them..." An idea hits me and my hands itch for my sketchbook, which is at home. I grab my phone and open my notes app. "Maybe we can make a special issue, one with the hospital kids as the superheroes. We can set up a fundraiser and give the issues to anyone who makes a donation. I'll talk to Slater."

His fingers wrap around my wrist, halting my typing. "I love the idea, but don't want to create more work for you."

"It's work I enjoy." I give him a quick kiss on the cheek because he's here, next to me, and I can, and I've been wanting to kiss him for weeks. After saving the note, I tuck my phone away. I do like the idea, and my excitement begins to build. Then an unwanted thought pops into my head. It *is* a lot of work. I'm not doing it to keep myself in Craig's orbit should he begin to slip away, am I?

I don't want to think about that possibility.

"I'm sorry I wasn't able to fly in yesterday. I hate breaking plans with you." Craig brings my free hand to his lips and brushes them over my knuckles, leaving a trail of tingles in their wake. "I wish I'd been here to start off your book's publication day with a celebration this morning. Starting with waking up with you."

"It's okay. You were busy. Plus, you sent me a very thoughtful present."

He scowls. "And your roommate ate the candy."

"When I watched him throw the empty box *with my name on it*, into the trash, I couldn't believe it. I wished I could channel one of our characters' powers and put him in his place. I'll get him back by making him a character in the next book who meets an unfortunate end."

He grins and kisses me. "You just got the cutest, evil genius smirk on your face."

"I'm thinking up ways to punish him on the page."

"I'm sure you'll think of something creative and fitting." His hand is a warm weight on my low back as we reach the bar. He orders a superhero cocktail for himself and gets me another villain one. Taking a taste of his, he surveys the people milling through the room. "I know Slater and Noah play for the Bedlam, but it's a little bizarre seeing so many of their teammates. I mean, we watch these guys in action at the arena or through our TVs, and here they are. Whoa, Devon is talking to Celek?"

I sip my drink, savoring the sweetness of the honey, the champagne bubbles tingling my tongue, and the smooth burn of the whiskey. "I introduced them. They're still chatting?

That's great. What about Cody?" Turning, I peer into the crowd.

Cody stands squaring off against Patrick, gazes locked on each other, the light of battle in their eyes. He gestures with his drink as he talks. Or is this a debate or argument? Patrick shakes his head and responds with something that makes Cody huff, but then he presents Cody with one of the mini sub sandwiches from his plate, and Cody accepts with a beaming smile.

"They have an interesting dynamic," I say.

Cup at his lips, Craig snorts into his drink. "To say the least."

In the front of the room, Noah claps his hands together, and waves to catch everyone's attention. "Thank you all for coming tonight and celebrating Slater and Ty's superhero series. One of the main characters is a hockey player. And we all know hockey players are superheroes, right?"

His Bedlam teammates cheer.

Noah grins. "They've put in a ton of long hours and hard work. Slater and Ty, we're proud of you and know this is only the beginning." He raises his glass. "To Slater and Ty."

"Slater and Ty." The words echo back. Craig taps his glass against mine, then bends and kisses me. The warmth from his kiss is better than any of the warmth from the alcohol circulating in my system.

I drain my glass and one of the Bedlam players near the bar gets me another. I'm feeling pleasantly buzzed. Cody and Patrick join us and Craig chats with them as I lean against him, content to stay in the circle of his embrace.

Soft lips brush my temple. "How many of those drinks have you had?"

"Three? No, wait. Four?" I shrug out of my jacket, then pluck my shirt from my chest, fanning the fabric, but it does nothing to cool me down. When did the room get so warm?

"When's the last time you ate anything?"

"I had a cookie right before Cody and Devon arrived."

"We need to get some food into you." Craig hugs me tighter to his chest.

Cody sets his glass on the table. "They're cutting the cake. I'll grab some slices. Paddy, help me? Ty probably needs a sandwich or something too."

The pair walk away. I tip my head back and kiss the scar on Craig's chin. "Your friends are nice."

"I like them."

The room's noise level rises as the event staff pass out plates of cake. Cody and Patrick return with a plate of sandwiches and another of cake. Cody also sets a glass of water beside me. The next time I look up, they're gone.

With one arm around me, Craig feeds me a bite of the chocolate raspberry goodness, then takes another for himself.

I snuggle in, playing with the bands in his bracelet. Maybe I'm picking up his nervous habit. "I'm really happy you're here."

He licks frosting from his lower lip and feeds me another bite. "I wouldn't have missed this for anything."

"No?" Looking at the cake remaining on the plate is easier than looking into his eyes. The room is still too warm and too loud, and I'm too buzzed to have this conversation. But emotions are welling up and I can't stop myself from talking. "Things seem like they're changing, and I'm scared those changes will drift us further apart. I don't want that to happen."

"Neither do I." His fingers touch my chin and raise my face to meet his serious gaze. "We won't let it."

"I want to believe that." All around us are pictures of

superheroes. Somehow, those heroes always find a way, no matter the odds stacked against them. "I wish superpowers were a real thing so I could see you anytime I wanted."

"I wish I had them too. It would make things much easier." Craig sets the plate down then cups my face in his hands. The intensity in his eyes takes my breath away. "You matter to me, Ty. That's not changing."

"You matter to me so much, it's scary." Burying my face in his neck, I draw his scent into my lungs. "I'm happy you're coming home with me tonight. We're staying at Slater and Noah's instead of my place. I want to go to sleep and wake up holding you." I raise my head and look into the eyes I've longed to see up close for weeks. "Not just want it. I need it."

His arms band around me, cradling me against his body. "I need it too."

CHAPTER TEN
CRAIG

Music, *our* music, swirls around me, filling the air of Devon's basement. Nodding along to the beat Devon and Patrick established, I improvise a riff to accompany it and harmonize with Cody's soulful voice. The song we've been working on for the past two hours is finally coming together.

I woke up wrapped around Ty, with new lyrics on the brain, this morning. The book launch party last night, and the things we'd said to each other, about how we matter to each other, have been on my mind too. After Ty went to work, I called Devon, Patrick, and Cody, and we've spent the first full day of my visit to Buffalo in this basement.

Devon's basement is a far cry from the studios I've grown used to in LA, but it was the site of our practice sessions before the move to LA, and has been our place for jam sessions in the years we've been apart. New sound-proofing material lines the gray-painted walls, and new chairs flank the overstuffed couch behind Devon's drum kit, but the framed concert posters lining one wall and the set-up of us four band members are exactly the same as always.

With Falling Midnight gaining an avalanche of social media followers since signing with Furious Records, thanks to *Better Days Ahead* going viral, there's a tension circulating within me, a pins and needles, walking on eggshells tension, like I'm holding my breath and afraid to exhale.

We have a signed contract. We almost have enough material to get into the studio and record our first album under the new label. And we have the upcoming tour with Satyr's Kiss. All four of us feel the pressure.

The song comes to a close, then I play the riff again. "What do you think?"

Head tilted to the side, Patrick stifles a yawn and gestures for me to repeat the riff. I do, and he nods. "Yeah. That's the one."

His yawn sets off mine. Life has been a whirlwind since my time on tour with Luke and the guys. From signing the contract, recording the duet with Luke and the studio session of *Better Days Ahead* with my band, then meetings with artists for songwriting projects, visits for the foundation, and songwriting for the new album, I'm exhausted. I need to lose myself in Ty, and I'll get to do that again tonight. Holding him last night was amazing, and I want more.

I've missed texting with him and talking with him as much as I used to before we signed with the label and life became a whirlwind. I don't want him slipping away, or feeling like he's not a priority for me. Because he is.

I'd hoped that my showing up to his book launch last night proved it, but one gesture isn't enough. Plus, I was a day late in arriving, thanks to work. Maybe if I'd been there when the flowers and candy delivery happened, Ty's awful roommate wouldn't have helped himself to the treats.

Seeing Ty via a screen and hearing him via a sound piece

isn't good enough. Neither is sporadic, in-person visits. I need a lot more of holding-him-close visits.

Much more than long weekends and stolen moments.

That thought has been turning over and over in my mind for weeks. My heartbeat stutters and I take a deep breath. "I'm thinking I might buy or rent a place here and be bi-coastal."

Three expressions of surprise and confusion mirror each other, and for a moment, no one speaks or moves, they only stare at me. My blurting that out with zero context might be why.

"You're moving here?" Devon bites his lip and then frowns at the drums. "Well, that changes things a bit."

"What do you mean?" I move closer.

He raises his gaze. "I've decided I'm moving back to LA. We have the contract and I know we're going there to record, but that's not enough. I let what happened with Anthony run me out of there, and I've regretted it for years. I want to go back. If I leave again, it'll be on my own terms. But I need to do this."

"Wow, Dev." Cody's voice is soft and his eyes glitter with sympathy.

Devon runs his hand over his face and then through his hair. "I talked to my regional manager. She said I could transfer to our flagship store in LA. I told her I'd need to cut back my hours to accommodate the tour, and she said it isn't a problem."

Cody sets the mic on the stand. "What about Celek? You two looked like you really hit it off last night."

"What about him?" Devon shrugs like the man doesn't matter, but wraps his arms around his middle, hugging himself. "We had a good conversation at the party, then we drifted apart during the chaos of people moving toward the food when the cake was cut. I looked for him after that, but one of his teammates said Celek left to drive another teammate who had a migraine home. Apparently, the guy was puking in the alley behind the gallery. He's a good captain, looking out for his teammates. He probably stayed with the guy and got him settled."

Cody props his elbow on the mic and looks at our friend, who is currently doing a lousy job of hiding his feelings. "Sorry, Dev."

It was good seeing Devon open and clearly enjoying the company of Celek at the party. After Anthony, none of us were sure he'd ever get back out there. So, if there's any way I can help him, I will. "I could ask Ty to give him your number."

He runs his finger along the curved edge of one of the cymbals. "I don't know. I mean, I'm going to LA, and he's here, and that would put us in the same situation you're in with Ty. I've seen how hard it's been on you, and I don't think I'm equipped for it."

"I understand, bud. It sucks, and I'm done with it. I need to be where he is, a lot more often than I have been." Tossing my guitar pick into the open case, I watch it land on the soft golden fabric. Everything I've ever wanted is within my reach. I just need to figure out how to put the pieces together. "What's that saying about falling in love making fools out of people?"

"Love? You're in love with him?" A smile beams across Devon's face, chasing away the gray clouds hanging over his expression. "Dude, that's awesome."

"So great." Cody presses his hands over his heart. "We love Ty. You two are perfect together. I completely understand you needing to be here with him. Now that you're in a relationship, will we be doing more love songs? Your lyrics might lean that way." His gaze flies to where Patrick sits on the stool across the room. "We'll have to rely on Paddy for the raw angst and biting lyrics."

Patrick's eyes flash and he raises one dark brow. "You know I hate when you call me that."

"No." Dragging the word out to one long syllable, Cody crosses his arms over his chest and lifts his chin. His eyebrow piercing glints in the overhead light. "I think you secretly love it. Just like you secretly love me."

"You're delusional."

"And you're in denial."

The clash of drumsticks hitting the crash cymbals reverberates through the air, and we all wince. Devon stands and points one wooden stick at Cody and Patrick. "The two of you, *enough.* Craig, are you serious about this?"

Nerves and exhilaration flow through me. Unsure how to word my thoughts, I play a chord, focusing on my fingers moving over the strings. "I am. I need more time with Ty. Long distance sucks. I'm tired of being three hours behind and three thousand miles apart."

"Understandable." Cody grabs a bottle of water from the shelf behind him. "Have you spoken to him about your decision yet?"

I shake my head and continue playing. "No. I thought I'd talk to him about it tonight. We're meeting up for dinner."

Water sloshes in the bottle as Cody turns it over and over. "When do *we* get to see Ty again?"

"Not for a few days at least. Maybe not for the whole visit. I might keep him to myself this time."

"Why?" Clutching the bottle to his chest, Cody blinks at me, all innocence. No one does wide-eyed shock better. My friend's theatrical talents are put to use on-stage and off. "Afraid we'll scare him away for good?"

"No. But the past two times we saw each other in person there were a lot of other people around, so I'm feeling pretty selfish about sharing him with anyone else. I had to share him last night at the book launch, too." Thinking about dinner leads to thinking about *afterwards*, and I need to establish some possible plans. "Devon... He has difficult roommates and their house is pretty cramped, so he's been staying with Slater and Noah. I don't know if we'll end up back at their place again, or here."

"Okay." Devon twirls his drumsticks through the fingers of both hands simultaneously, a move he mastered back when we were in high school. "Hold on. Are you actually asking for my permission to bring someone home?"

"No." Then I stop and think about it. "Actually, yeah. If I bring Ty back here to spend the night, would you think I'm an inconsiderate houseguest?"

"No way. Ty's welcome. And my bedroom is far enough away from the guest room that I shouldn't hear anything, if you were worried about that."

"Can I stay over too?" Eyes brimming with laughter and smile a mile wide, Cody falls to his knees in front of Devon's drum kit and raises his hands in a pleading pose. "We love Ty, and you two together are couple goals. I'll even serve you guys breakfast in bed."

Cracking up at his antics, I reach over and ruffle his hair, mussing the dark strands. "What about your own houseguest?"

Patrick sets the bass aside. He strides past Cody and swipes another bottle of water. "His houseguest would be fine with some peace and quiet."

The laughter and smile fade as Cody's features cloud with hurt. He stands, brushing off his jeans. "You don't have to stay with me, Paddy, if I'm too much for you. Get a hotel room, or sleep outside, or go back to LA early. Whatever. I don't care."

"*Guys*. We've been together for less than twenty-four hours." Exasperation fills Devon's voice. A thunderous look darkening his face, he holds his drumsticks above the crash cymbals, letting the threat hang. "Stop. Or I'll call an end to practice right now."

My concern grows as I study the pair. Patrick seems pissed off, and Cody's hurt isn't an act. I don't understand Patrick's change in mood, but he and Cody can turn a one-eighty, going from getting along to not, in a flash. "Guys—"

"Call it. I think I'm about done anyway." Gaze still wounded, Cody raises a hand to his throat. "I need tea. And food. Anyone hungry?"

Without waiting for a response, he jogs up the stairs. The door at the top leads to the kitchen. He lets it slam behind him.

"Damn it." Devon sets the sticks down, then leaps out of his seat. Striding through the room, he levels a glare at Patrick. "Why you're staying with him and why he asked you is beyond me. You're like oil and vinegar. And speaking of that, I need to check on him. Last time he got upset, he made an absolute fucking mess of my kitchen."

He heads up the steps. The door slams a second time with his exit. Silence fills the space, as heavy as the tension-filled interactions.

Hands tucked into his front pockets, Patrick leans against the wall. A scowl darkening his features, he stares at the poster advertising our first gig, gazing at something in the print, or perhaps so caught up in his thoughts that he isn't focusing on anything in particular.

I remove my guitar and set it against the case. Treading in the waters of the Patrick and Cody situation has the potential to be explosive. Over the years, Devon and I have become masters at getting the guys to talk, or make up, or see reason, and smooth ruffled feathers.

Moving around the room, I unplug cords and wrap up wires. "What did you guys do this morning before you came over?"

"Not much. Watched some show Cody likes. He made me breakfast."

"In bed?" I can't help teasing, thinking of Cody's earlier offer.

Finally, Patrick's scrutiny swings in my direction. His expression is unreadable. "No."

"Did you fight? You both seemed fine before we started playing."

His gaze shoots to the microphone, then to the closed door. "Contrary to popular belief, we don't fight all the time."

"Just most of it?"

With a sigh, Patrick pushes away from the wall. "What do you want, Craig?"

"I want to know why you're acting this way." Legs splayed, I cross my arms over my chest and wait. I can out-stubborn the man. "We have a second shot at our dream, and this time, with the support of Furious Records, it can actually come true. We should all be getting along, not fighting. So, what gives? Are you regretting giving this a go?"

"No. Put it down to me being exhausted and jet-lagged, and agreeing to spend the next two weeks rooming with someone who gets under my skin like no one else." He twists the cap off the water bottle. "I'm sorry I'm being an ass. I'll apologize to him."

"Want to switch with me? You can stay here and I'll stay with Cody. I'll probably end up staying with Ty most nights anyway."

"No. It's fine."

"If you're sure..." We watch each other and I can't help feeling there's something he's not telling me. Hopefully, he'll feel he can open up and share soon. I don't like knowing one of my best friends is out of sorts, but I can't force the man to spill his secrets. "You haven't said anything about me maybe living here part-time."

His brows shoot up. "It's your life. You can do whatever you want. To echo Devon's earlier question, are you asking for my permission?"

"Of course not. But I don't want to leave you stranded. It's been the two of us together in the same city for a decade."

Patrick immediately shakes his head. "You're not abandoning me. Plus, we'll be seeing each other more with all the band stuff. I'll be fine."

"Are you sure?"

"You've found someone who makes you happy." His voice softens along with his expression, erasing all evidence of the earlier scowls and tension. "You haven't been happy the last few years, buddy. Not like how you are with Ty. You should be where he is as often as possible."

"There's so much to think about. The band has commitments and obligations now. I want to be where you guys are. But I want to be with him too."

"We'll make things work." He lets that thought hang, and I know he's right.

"I know we will." My voice is sure. "I've always been happiest when we're jamming together."

He takes a swig of water. "Then you met Ty, and now you're happiest with him. Don't deny it. Our feelings won't be hurt that someone's displaced us."

"Not displaced."

"In a way, we have been. But it's okay. You found your person."

"Yeah. I have."

He smiles at me, then pulls a face and rolls his eyes. "Okay, enough mushy shit. When you're here, if music or lyrics come to you, or to us, we'll record the sessions and send them to each other, attempt more virtual rehearsing. But we'll need to see each other often so we can play together. You keeping your apartment in LA?"

"Yeah. Maybe Devon can stay there when I'm not." I pull out my phone and open my notes app, making a list of the things I need to do. "I also have to talk to the people at the foundation… What do you think about me starting up a branch of it here in Buffalo?"

"That's a good idea." He sets the bottle down, then picks it up again and wanders toward the mic stand. "Having Dev with me will be awesome. I'm glad he's moving back. Wish he'd never gone away. Cody too. LA won't be the same without you. It'll be better when we're all there together."

Feeling the warm glow of friendship, I bump our shoulders together. "You know, you could always spend more time here with me…"

"Yeah, I don't think so." Patrick shakes his head, but he's smiling. "Visits are fine, but I'm not moving back."

"I get it." We'll figure everything out. I'm determined to have it all. My friends, my band, and Ty.

The door at the top of the stairs swings open, and Cody comes halfway down the steps. "I'm leaving. Craig, have a great time with Ty tonight. Tell him we said hi. See you at practice tomorrow. *Patrick*, if you decide to stay elsewhere, please let me know so I can lock up properly and make sure you return my key."

"Cody, wait." Looking contrite, Patrick cuts a path through the room. "I'm sorry for what I said earlier."

The hoop in his brow glinting in the overhead light, Cody eyes him warily. "All right."

"I mean it." He meets him on the stairs and lays a hand on our shorter friend's shoulder. "I was out of line. Can I still stay with you?"

Cody's gaze bounces from Patrick's face to where his hand rests and back again. Hurt still haunts his features. "I'm not too extra for you?"

"You're just the right amount of extra." Warmth tinges Patrick's words and affectionate tone.

I slowly tread closer to the guys. It seems we all hold our collective breath as Cody wages an internal debate. If I have to play referee again so soon...

Finally, Cody nods. "You can stay."

Devon appears in the doorway, holding a steaming mug. The scent of coffee drifts toward me. "Glad everyone's friends again. Let's try to keep it that way. Hey, Craig, I think I might keep this house as a rental property. You could stay here when you're in town."

"That works out. I was thinking you could stay at my apartment in LA when I'm here." I tuck my phone in my pocket. "But I wonder if Ty might like visiting LA more often. I hope we can spend more time there together."

With a dramatic sigh, Cody sags against the railing. His black nail polish is a stark contrast to the white painted wood. "Well, if you're all going to be in LA, I don't want to be the only one here."

"Wait, you want to move back to LA?" Patrick gapes at Cody. But there's more behind his gaze, like maybe everything he wants is within his grasp.

"If we're getting a chance to relive our dream, and you're

all going to be there together, at least for half a year, if Craig splits his time evenly, then I don't want to be left out, missing out on things again."

"I get that." And I do. He was the first to leave, and had to listen to us talking about practices and gigs, band drama and trauma, setting aside his dreams to take care of his dad. He deserves to experience every single second of this opportunity.

"My dad's not sick anymore. He's been dating Sylvia for two years, so I don't have to worry about him being alone, or feel like I'd be abandoning him." Cody frowns at the mic stand, his brows drawing together in concentration. "I don't want to deal with being a landlord. I can sell my house, hopefully find someplace to rent in LA, and then maybe when I come back here for visits, I can stay at Devon's." He glances at me. "Would you mind if we were here at the same time?"

"Fine with me." It all seems so easy, and eagerness bubbles up inside of me. Eagerness to see where our band goes. Eagerness to be with the men who have been such an important part of my life for so long. Eagerness to have something real, something more with Ty.

Devon's expression takes on the same animated glee as when we first moved out to California. "We could rent a place in LA together."

Cody's head bobs up and down with enthusiasm as his smile threatens to take over his entire face. The tension in his shoulders dissolves. "I'd like that."

My head feels like it's spinning. I went from telling them I think I need to be bi-coastal for my relationship, and now both Devon and Cody are moving to LA. If I could have Ty there too, then all the most important people in my life would be in one place.

Devon takes another sip from his mug. "I know you've

been in my house a million times, but if you do end up living here, you might want to look at it again through fresh eyes. Want to do that now?"

"Sure." I've always liked the feel of his home. Even more so with the renovations he did after he bought the house from his parents when they moved to a retirement community in Las Vegas. "Let's do it."

"We'll come too." Cody's voice rings out, accompanied by a flourish as he gestures at himself and Patrick. Then he glances at Patrick, lowers his arm, and his shoulders round as he shifts to a lower step. "Unless you want to go yourself, Craig, and just walk through with Devon."

Needing to fix the still-healing wound, I clamp a hand on both Patrick's and Cody's shoulders. "Are you kidding? I need all of you with me. Plus, if you're staying here on visits, you need to decide where you'd want to sleep."

We climb the steps to the first floor. The house, the only one on the block that has three stories, doesn't fit with the styles of the rest of the split-levels on the street. It's unique.

Devon stops by the coffee pot and tops off his mug. Either he or Cody set out three other mugs when they were up here earlier. "I had a new roof put on last year and a new HVAC system. The appliances are only a few years old, and the hardwood floors are in great shape."

All fine and good, but I'm more drawn to the carved moldings, hidden pocket doors, and the natural light spilling into every room. The house has charm and character.

I walk into the dining room, but can easily see the space converting to a music room. Having my piano along the far wall. The guitars and amps set on one side, and space for a desk and a comfortable chair.

One door down is the room Devon uses as an office. Light spills in from large windows on three sides, bathing the room in brightness, perfect for Ty to create art. I can picture him huddling over a drafting table. Sketching. Painting. Being there. Sharing my space. "It's perfect."

Patrick turns away from his study of the room and slings his arm over Cody's shoulder. "Yeah, I can picture the two of you here."

Anxious to share this with Ty, my fingers itch to grab my phone and call him. "The music room and this one here are what really matter."

Cody tentatively rests his head on Patrick's shoulder, and relaxes degree by degree, until he's leaning against Patrick's side. "You should bring Ty over. Let him get a feel for the space."

"You're right." I can picture us cooking in the bright kitchen, sharing a spacious shower in the primary bedroom and soaking together in the clawfoot tub.

Finished touring the rooms, we step outside. I walk onto the front lawn and stare up at the house, my memories of visiting Devon and jamming here mixing in with my visions for the future. "It's a great house, Dev. I'll take care of it while I'm here. And I can't wait for us all to be together in LA too. And on the road, sharing the stage."

He joins me and loops an arm around my shoulder, looking at the place that's been his home for most of his life. "Big changes coming for all of us."

"Yeah. Hopefully, they go the way we want." The cheerful flowers bobbing in the window boxes seem like they're rooting for me. Ty had to work this morning, then is visiting the comic book store with Slater and Noah this afternoon. I pull out my phone and glance at the time. They might be there now.

A text alert beeps, and I open the message and grin. Another sign that this is the right thing to do. I have a legitimate reason for visiting the comic book store now. Maybe I'll run into them there. I don't know if I'll be able to wait until tonight to see Ty.

As with my band, my relationship with him feels like it was meant to be. And I don't want to wait another second without telling the man exactly how I feel. I only wish I'd told him sooner.

CHAPTER ELEVEN
TY

I flip through the row of colorful comic books, my gaze jumping between the titles in my stack and the ones Slater is scanning by my side. Our weekly meeting at the comic book store to buy new issues has an added bonus competition to see who can find the most new artists to try out. The display of our books on a table near the window, with a sign noting *local authors*, is a thrill to see. I hope people give our book a chance.

We're still riding high from the launch. The Bedlam's media relations department mentioned the book on the team's social media sites and the hockey league picked up the story, and is running it on their website and social media too. They've asked us to do an interview that will run during one of the nationally televised games this fall. The wave feels like it's growing, and I wonder if this overwhelmed and exhilarated feeling is similar to what Craig and his bandmates are experiencing with their surge of success.

A soft stream of music echoes from the store's speakers. Aside from the few patrons scattered throughout the space, Slater and I have the back of the store to ourselves. To get the best selection, we time our visits to occur on delivery day, straight after Slater and Noah finish with hockey practice. Even during the off-season, we stick to this schedule, and hit the store once their daily training is complete.

"Guys," Noah approaches us with a to-go cup of tea in one hand. "I was talking to the owner. He said the stacks of your books on that table are the last from the five boxes he bought. They sold out of the rest."

"That's awesome." I high-five Slater, and he grins. His audience has really come through for us. Turning back to the comics, I spy a special anniversary collection of the caped crusader on an end cap, and my thoughts shift to Craig. But then again, I think about Craig every single day.

Slater jerks his head toward the comic. "I can't see that character without being reminded of Craig."

"Same." Heat flashes into my chest at the memory of waking up wrapped in his arms this morning. I want that every day. "We're having dinner together tonight. He's been working hard with the band all day. I thought I'd take him to that Mexican place we went to last month."

"Did you decide when you're going to talk to him?" Slater pauses his flipping, pulls out a book and scans it, but returns it and continues flipping through the titles.

I keep my attention on the books I'm sorting through. "We talked about it a little bit last night, but I was too buzzed and sleepy for a real conversation. So, hopefully tonight. I'm a little nervous, but I don't want to put it off."

A triumphant smile bursts onto Slater's face. After giving me a series of enthusiastic pats on the back, he wraps his arm around Noah's shoulders and pulls his boyfriend in close. "Good."

'Ty…" Noah's thoughtful tone goes no further.

My fingers needling the strap of the bag holding my sketchbook, I turn away from the wall of books. "What?"

"Craig's here."

"Here?" I whirl to face the direction Noah points me in.

Craig's tall form strides through the store, his long strides eating up the distance. "Hey, guys."

Slater waves, tucking Noah against his side. "Good to see you."

"I'm glad you're still here." Craig stands before me, clad in blue jeans, sneakers, and a gray T-shirt. He's holding a bag with the store's logo on it. "I got a call that my special order came in. Check it out."

He unearths a black T-shirt from the bag and holds it up. The image of our comic book's supervillain is across the chest. On the reverse side is the villain's shield, and below it, the logo of our series. I designed the merch, and we've partnered with the store to sell it on our behalf, but this is the first time I've seen our product in someone else's hands.

Slater leans in for a closer inspection. "The quality's the same as the samples we approved. Thanks for the brand rep, Craig, we appreciate it."

I'm a messy swirl of surprise and happiness. "You bought the villain!"

"Told you I would." He glances at the figure. "He looks good. A complex character, much like his creator."

Holding tighter to the strap on my bag, I scoff at him. "I'm not that complex."

"How about captivating?" He steps into my space, swoops in, kisses me, and wraps me in his arms. "Can't argue with captivating."

"Can't I?" I nip his lip.

Chuckling, he traces his thumb along my jawline. "I'm

happy to spend hours convincing you how captivating I find you."

"We get hours together? Yes, please." The prospect of several uninterrupted hours is what I'm craving.

"We'll have a lot more of that soon. I've decided to be bi-coastal." Something I can't name swirls in those brown eyes and there's a catch in his voice, and an extra gentleness in the way he holds me. "Split my time between here and LA. And whatever touring comes up."

Surprise mixes with disbelief and I shift back until I can clearly see Craig's earnest, serious expression and kind eyes. I rest my hands on his strong shoulders. "You're moving here part-time? But I thought you said weeks ago, the night at the hotel lounge, that Devon might move to LA?"

"He is moving there. Cody's going now too. But you aren't there. I want to be where you are." The way Craig smiles and threads his fingers through my hair erases all my worries. "Short of splitting myself in two, this is the way to make that happen."

I swallow against my thickening throat and the threat of tears pricking the backs of my eyes. "I can't believe it."

He sweeps his hand back down and continues stroking my cheek. "I meant it when I told you there isn't much I wouldn't do for you."

"So did I." Happiness spins through me as the world shifts from muted, muddied grays into a brilliant rainbow of colors. I place my hand over Craig's heart. I now know what I need to do. What I want to do. What I was afraid to ask for before, when this was more up in the air. "The fact that you would've moved here means so much to me, but it makes more sense for me to move to LA. I don't *have* to stay here. You need to be there. Your band is there. So's the foundation."

The softest, sweetest expression crosses Craig's face. He sucks in a breath. "You'd do that for me?"

"Absolutely. I want to. I need to be where you are." Leaning into his touch, I soak it up. "Long distance is hard. We're both busy. I was afraid I'd lose you."

"No way that's happening."

Smiling, I kiss his palm. "I'll need to find a job and an apartment."

"You can stay with me." He bends so our foreheads rest together. We breathe each other in. The touch and scent of him grounds me. "We're hiring you to do our album artwork. I'll help you find a job, get set up for freelancing, whatever you need."

More and more good feelings wrap around me, weaving us tighter together. I bask in it. And in him.

Movement in the corner of my vision alerts me to my friends watching us. I release my hold, wait for Craig to do the same, then step back. "I'd still need to come here to visit Slater and Noah, and we have more comic books to bring to life."

With his arm slung around Noah's shoulders, Slater beams at me, his blue eyes twinkling. "We can work together virtually. Video chats, so it's like you're sitting across from me in the kitchen. But yeah, we need in-person visits, too." His gaze shoots to Craig. "Ty's our family."

Tears prick my eyes again, and I swallow hard at the protectiveness of Slater's declaration. It's what I imagined having a brother would be like. "You're my family too."

He and Noah both grin, and Slater pulls me toward them. He hugs me and Noah squeezes my shoulder. I'm beyond lucky to have them.

The bag in his hand crinkles when Craig slips his T-shirt

inside it. As soon as Slater releases me, Craig tucks me into his side, like he never wants to let go. "You're welcome to visit us anytime you're in LA."

"We'll take you up on that," Noah pulls Craig into a hug, slapping his back, and I think I hear, "Take good care of him," before he releases my man.

Craig shifts closer, until we're touching once more. His fingers skate along my arm from my hand to my shoulder and back again. "Maybe you'd want to join me volunteering with the foundation again? I think the kids would like seeing a villain show up. Batman apprehending the Joker. Thor capturing Loki. Or, maybe you could be a superhero once in a while too. What do you say?"

"One hundred percent yes, I'm in. I'd love that."

Slater clears his throat. "If you need any other volunteers in the off-season, Craig, count us in. Noah and I still have the superhero costumes we wore last Halloween."

I glance at Slater and Noah, smile, and gesture toward my friends as I say to Craig, "These guys visit the hospital a lot, representing the Bedlam. The kids always light up seeing them." Turning to Slater and Noah, I continue, "I'd love to have you guys visiting with us, superhero style."

"It would be fun." Noah sips his tea and the faint scent of mint wafts my way. "You can also count on us for a donation."

Craig shakes both their hands. "That's awesome, guys. Thanks."

"No problem." Slater grabs Noah's arm and tugs his boyfriend forward. "We'll get out of your way now, let you talk more. Ty, we'll see you at home. Craig, I'm glad you're here and that you guys have worked things out."

And then my friends are gone.

I grip the strap on my bag as I stare at Craig. Part of me still can't believe this man was ready to uproot his life for me. But maybe I can, since I'm ready to do the same thing. "So... I'm moving to LA."

He nods and smiles. "Big changes."

My heartbeat flutters faster as the reality of my decision fully sinks in. I think about his offer for me to stay with him. It's where I want to be. "The biggest. Are we changing too?"

His fingers twisting the leather strap encircling his wrist, Craig bites his lip and his searching gaze roams my face. "The past two months, really getting to know you, has been incredible. I've never felt this way about anyone before, Ty. I want to call you my boyfriend. To keep exploring what we have together. To experience more with each other. To be there to support each other through the good and the bad and everything in between."

There's an ache in my chest, a yearning for everything he's said. "I want all of that."

He releases a breath and his hold on the bracelet, and there's an ease in his movements as he slides his arm around my shoulders. "Good."

I grab my sketchbook, the one I bought with him in LA, from my bag. "I want to show you something. How often you've been on my mind since we met. I got this book that day. It's filled with you. Us."

Craig flips through the book. Sketches of him dressed as Batman, and the two of us in our costumes visiting the foundation are first. Followed by more sketches of Craig with his guitar on stage and at home, another of him sitting at his piano, and another of him in the hotel room's bed. There's a sketch of us at the beach. One of our hands linked together. And the final image is of the two of us together in an embrace, sketched from a photo Slater took at the launch party.

He traces his finger over the page. "I love them all, but that last one is my favorite."

"Mine too." I quickly tuck away the sketchbook, and then grasp Craig's hand. "I've fallen faster for you than anyone ever."

He slowly draws me against his chest. "It was a free-fall for me from the moment we met, and I've never been happier."

Our lips touch, and the connection radiates throughout my body. I slide my arms around my boyfriend and hold tight. In the circle of his embrace, everything seems brighter and better, in my world and in my heart.

After a long moment, Craig lifts his head. "On my way here, I was thinking about us staying at Devon's house and how we could use the rooms, where you'd draw and I'd create music. I walked through it with the guys, and could see everything so clearly. But now, I'm thinking about my apartment in LA and how I can rearrange the music room at home. Create a spot for you that gets great lighting by the windows. I can picture you sketching there at a drafting table or on a couch, and me writing lyrics or playing my guitar or piano and looking up and seeing you there, sharing my space."

Planning a future for us together, I wholeheartedly approve. "I can't wait to share it with you."

Smiling, Craig strokes his fingers along my back. "Cody, Patrick, and Devon will be stoked it worked out this way. You have no idea what this means to me."

"I think I have some idea." The depth of my emotions for him catches in my throat. I clear it, and I'm sure what I feel for him is shining in my eyes. "After all, you were ready to uproot your life for me."

"Totally worth it." He trails his fingers through my hair, and everything in his gaze tells me this is real, and this will last. "Ready to go share our news with them?"

I stretch up and kiss him again, sharing all of the hope, enthusiasm, and happiness overflowing from my heart. "I'm ready for anything."

CHAPTER TWELVE
TY

"Two beers." I raise my voice, competing with the pulsing music and conversations from the costumed partygoers crowding the bar. My reflection in the mirrored wall behind the bar catches my attention. The Riddler costume is new, fits me perfectly, and is a good match for Craig's Batman. I love the way we look together. Even though we didn't win the couples costume contest.

While I wait for the drinks, I scan the room. Strands of orange twinkling lights crisscross the ceiling in a spider web pattern. Glittery purple bats and orange pumpkins hang at various heights from wires. Bowls in the shape of shiny black cauldrons containing mixtures of candy are spread throughout the room.

The Halloween party, a fundraiser hosted by the comic book store to support art lessons at the local community center, grows in size every year. With the upcoming move to LA, I wonder if I'll be back here for next year's party, or if we'll start a new tradition in LA.

I pay, waving for the bartender to keep the change, then collect the cold bottles and weave my way through the crowd.

There are a few witches, zombies, and scary clowns, but for the most part, the attendees' outfits span the wide array of comic book universe characters.

A huge, neon orange Happy Halloween sign hanging on the white brick wall casts a warm glow over my group of friends. Slater and Noah, who won the couples contest dressed as Superman and Lex Luthor, chat with Craig, Devon, Cody, and Patrick.

Craig glances up from his conversation with Slater and welcomes me with a smile and an arm around my waist. "Thanks for the drink."

Cradling my beer, I lean into his side. In the costume, my boyfriend is as dashing as the very first time I saw him. "What did I miss?"

"Nothing. Just chatting about the hockey game."

"It was a great one." Craig and I, along with Devon, attended the action-packed afternoon game with tickets Slater and Noah gifted us. The entire game had been a flurry of flying pucks and flying fists. Noah scored two goals, Slater won a fight, and the team got the win. The conclusion of the first month of hockey season has the Bedlam sitting at the top of the standings.

Slater pauses in the act of peeling the purple foil wrapper away from a piece of chocolate candy. "I'm glad the game was this afternoon and not tonight. Between hockey games and practices for us, Craig's band going on tour, and you guys getting ready for the move to LA, we've barely seen you this month."

"Considering I'm staying down the hall from you, that's saying something." I've been living with them since they issued the invitation to me the night of the launch party. They're amazing friends I'm going to miss like crazy.

They kept me distracted and entertained while Craig and

his band traveled with Satyr's Kiss for their shows at the beginning of the month. Slater and I worked on drawing his teammates into a comic strip for our holiday present and I attended my last in-person Bedlam book club meeting. The guys said they could add a virtual option for me so I can keep taking part.

The last two weeks have been especially busy. Most of my things were in boxes already, from my move from the house I'd shared with my old roommates to Slater and Noah's place. But I was finishing up my last few weeks at the insurance company and also helping Devon and Cody box things up for our official move to LA.

Though he'd gone back to LA for a few weeks to handle some projects with other artists, Craig's been here in Buffalo helping us for the past five days. I can't wait to get settled in his apartment, and to have Cody and Devon moved into Celek's beach house in Malibu. The pair are renting it from the Bedlam's team captain through an arrangement initiated by Slater, and though Devon swears nothing's going on between Celek and him, I know sparks when I see them.

My worry about finding a job in LA ended when Furious Records offered me a graphics design position I can do from anywhere, so I can be with Craig whether we're in LA or on the road touring. Working with the label and with their bands lets me stretch my creative muscles in new directions.

Rolling my shoulders, I feel the ache from lifting so many moving boxes. We finally finished packing everything for the guys. I nearly cried when Craig showed me a video of the space he'd created for me in his music room. The level of care and detail he'd taken in creating the art side of the room means the world to me. I feel welcomed, valued, and loved.

"I'm glad you guys could be here tonight. It means a lot to Ty and me." Craig bends and brushes his lips over my temple, right above the mask. "Thanks for letting us crash at your place."

Slater lays his hand on my shoulder. "Like we told you, that room is yours anytime you're in Buffalo. We're gonna miss you, Ty."

My eyes prick with the threat of tears. "You've been so good to me."

Noah wraps his arms around us both. "It'll be tough not having you down the hall from us, but we'll do video calls and see you when we're in LA for games. Maybe we'll run into you at away game cities when you travel with Craig."

I nod. "I know we'll see each other, but it won't be the same as before. More video. Less in person."

Slater hugs me. "Only until the summer. Then we'll join you in LA, crash Celek's beach house, and work on the next comic books. It'll be epic. Maybe we'll rent our own tour bus and follow Falling Midnight around, so we can hang out with all of you."

"I can't wait." Smiling, I squeeze him tight, then do the same to Noah. "Love you guys."

"We love you too." Noah presses a kiss to my cheek. "We're happy you're chasing your dreams. And that you won't be alone out there."

"Not alone. I'll have friends who look out for me just like you two do." Smiling, I gesture at the tight-knit trio who've welcomed me with enthusiasm and kindness, and celebrate my relationship with their oldest friend.

Cody, in his Captain America costume, gives me a salute. He's affixed a glow-in-the-dark pumpkin sticker to the star at the center of his chest and another on the shield he carries. "We'll always have Ty's back. That's a promise."

"Thanks, Cody. That means a lot to us. Let's get a picture

together. All of us." Slater holds up his phone and waves for everyone to gather in close.

"Super Squad, assemble." With a dramatic flourish, Cody raises his shield high above his head.

Chuckling, Patrick moves closer to the man, shaking his head. Lacking the mask and long hair, he still received compliments on his Winter Soldier costume. "Dude, that is *not* what they say. I should know, after sitting through that movie marathon with you guys last weekend."

His expression swinging from exasperation to amusement, Cody cocks his head to the side and slowly lowers the shield. The light of battle sparks in his gaze. "But we're not all dressed as Avengers, Paddy, so I'm improvising."

Devon, the lone rebel against the group's superhero theme, wields his light saber and steps between the bickering duo. His brown robe swishes as he moves. "You two *will* get along."

Laughing, I snuggle closer to Craig and whisper, "I really like your friends."

"Don't know what I'd do without them. And now all of us will be together in the same place. It's perfect." He shifts his position, sliding behind me, and wraps his other arm around my torso, enveloping me in warmth and strength. "Especially having you there."

"Back at you." I smile at our image reflected in Slater's phone. The rest of the group gathers in close and fills the screen. They are a good crew and I consider all of them part of my family.

After taking several photos, Slater lowers his phone. "I think we got some great shots. I'll share them with whoever wants the pics."

The group spreads out. Cody and Patrick head for the bar, promising to bring back refills for everyone, and Slater draws

Devon into a conversation with Noah about the next pick for the Bedlam book club.

I lean my head back and stretch until my lips graze Craig's jaw. "How's the tattoo feeling? Having any regrets about getting your narwhal covered?"

"Nope. It was time to bid it goodbye." His appointment with Noah's tattoo artist this afternoon brought the dragon tattoo to life on his skin. We worked on the design for the last month and a half, in between my other commissions and packing. The tattoo covers Craig's arm from his shoulder to his elbow. Of all the drawings I've done, the elaborate, fiery creature with music notes woven throughout the dragon's scales is one of my favorite pieces.

"I love seeing you sport the dragon. Still, I miss the narwhal a little."

"You do?"

I tap Craig's arm to loosen his hold, then turn and face him. Those arms come back around me, just as I knew they would. "For a silly, sentimental reason. They are the unicorns of the sea. And finding you was like finding a unicorn. As in, finding my perfect match."

Craig's hold tightens and his gaze crackles with an intensity that steals my breath. "Ty... There's something I have to say. Something I've been wanting to say for a while. If I wait anymore, I'm going to burst."

My grip on the icy beer tightens. I quickly set it down. My heartbeat thumps hard then kicks into higher gear. The air seems to still. Every sense heightens and every cell in my body vibrates with anticipation. I think I know what words might leave Craig's lips. Words I myself have been longing to say. "Craig?"

His tongue peeks out to wet his lips. Gloved fingers flex on my back, then roam in a soft caress. "I love you."

"I love you too." The words flow easily, automatically, and I mean them with every fiber of my being. They are a declaration and a commitment.

The most wondrous expression graces Craig's face, as if the knowledge his feelings are returned is the greatest, most monumental thing in the history of ever.

We stand, holding each other and smiling, wrapped in our private moment as the party continues around us. For a moment, I wish the masks weren't in place, so that nothing would hide even an inch of our expressions. I want to see all of Craig, and comfort myself with the plan of whispering *I love you* to him over and over as soon as we get back to my room at Slater and Noah's place.

Craig's teeth sink into his bottom lip, drawing my attention to his sexy mouth. "You love me."

"Yes." The word flies out, eager and certain. I cradle his cheek. "Absolutely. And I'm so ready to be with you. I want a life together."

"That's what we're building." Eyes twinkling, Craig grins and bends until our heads are close together. "I knew right away that you were special, and the months we've been together have let me see just how amazing. You're my partner. My perfect match. And most of all, my superhero."

Our lips meet and I press myself against Craig, sharing the promise held in the kiss. Happiness, pure and deep, radiates through me until I'm sure I glow as bright as the neon sign.

I've fallen fast for Craig. Faster than I'd ever fallen for anyone. But it doesn't surprise me. After all, love is the greatest, most potent superpower in the universe.

EPILOGUE
TY

One Year Later

In all the years I attended comic book conventions, I never dreamed I'd be selling my own comics at one. Yet here I am.

Slater and I have a table at the very convention where I met Craig one year ago. The sea of people and the volume of noise and chaos is the same, but so much else is different compared to my life back then.

The table for the superhero foundation is beside ours. I've been going back and forth between the tables, telling people about the foundation when the other volunteers are occupied, and then coming back to my table and chatting about comic books with customers and Slater and Noah. It's been a whirlwind of a day, but I'm happy.

Noah's playing the part of proud boyfriend for Slater, talking about the books, about literacy, and being a pro at selling our merch. The brightly colored tees, hats, mugs, and bags are flying off the tables as fast as copies of the original superhero series and the special edition we created to raise money for the foundation.

My own boyfriend has been in New York City for the past four days with Cody, Patrick, and Devon, opening for The Fury. I'd have gone with them if we didn't have the convention. Falling Midnight's new album is climbing the charts. They worked so hard on it and I'm thrilled for the guys. I've kept my promise to Craig about being their number one super fan. He smiles so big whenever I wear one of the hats or tees with their logo.

Slater hands a bulging bag to a customer who purchased one of everything, then turns to me. "It's surreal being back here."

"I know." I straighten the display copies of our books. "Being on the other side of the table is a different perspective."

Noah steps around to the customer side then raises his phone. "Lean in, you two. Smile."

Leaning into Slater, I smile for the camera. "Watch out for random boxes doubling as tripping hazards."

"Oh, don't worry, I did. But I'll check again." He does an exaggerated survey of the floor around him before taking the photos. We moved the boxes to behind our chairs instead of under the table to make sure there's no way a customer could trip.

Though I love living here in LA with Craig and his crew, I've missed having these two guys down the hall from me. I'm glad we have an entire summer together. Standing, I hold out my hand for his phone. "Let me take one of you guys."

Noah passes the phone to me. I squeeze between the tables and take his place in front of it and wait for him to claim the chair I vacated. Once he's seated, Slater wraps an arm around his shoulders and they lean in so their temples are touching. It's very cute.

I take a few pictures. "You guys look great, so I hope the

photos do too. Let me back up, get a wider angle so there's more of the convention in the shot."

Moving fast, I back up a few steps, and slam into something large and solid. In a split-second, last year's collision with the hard table and crashing into Craig's display flashes through my mind. Adrenaline spikes, and panic rolls through my gut.

Hands wrap around my shoulders from behind, stopping my fall, and steadying me.

"Careful, Ty." Craig's murmured voice hovers by my ear. Strong hands slip down to the bare skin below my T-shirt sleeve.

A thrill races through my body, sending my heart rate soaring and goosebumps dotting my skin.

I spin around.

Craig stands before me. As dashing as ever, clad in blue jeans, boots, and a T-shirt with my superhero's shield on his chest, he smiles. "Hi."

"You're back! You weren't supposed to be back until late tonight." I push into his arms and my whole being relaxes when they come around me, wrapping me in his strength and his cinnamon scent.

He presses kisses to my temple, cheek, then lips. "I missed you. So I hopped on an earlier flight."

"I'm happy you did. I'm not used to sleeping without you." My hands roam his back, and I pull him in, snuggling him closer to me. "How were the fans with the new song?"

"Enthusiastic." With his arm around me, he walks us to our table. "They loved it. Adding it to the set list was a good move."

We round the table and he greets Slater and Noah, then says hello to the foundation's volunteers. With our busy schedules, life often feels chaotic and like we're pulled in multiple directions. But once a month, we don costumes for the hospital visits. Craig's prediction several months ago was right, the kids love seeing Loki, and the other villains mixed in with the superheroes. In addition to playing the villains, I've been Robin to Craig's Batman twice, and Deadpool to his Wolverine.

Craig slips his arms around my waist and grins at Falling Midnight's logo on my chest. "How has today been?"

"Really good. We sold a lot of books. Slater and I were working on sketches for the new series yesterday and this morning. I'll show you later." I pet the tail of the dragon tattoo peeking out from beneath his short sleeve, something I've taken to doing whenever we stand like this. "I'll have plenty to keep me busy on the tour bus."

"Will I be on your list?" His gaze tender, he strokes his hand through my hair. "I plan on keeping you occupied. There are things we need to discuss."

"Such as?" I lean into the caresses.

"You and me and a vacation once the tour ends."

The tour kicks off next weekend with Falling Midnight playing several shows in California. Slater and Noah will be hanging out in Celek's beach house, which Cody and Devon still rent from the Bedlam captain, relaxing for a week before renting their own tour bus and joining us. There's a rumor Celek might come too. I'm not sure how Devon will react to that. The summer tour should be interesting.

Drawing in Craig's cinnamon scent, I hook my finger through his belt loop and rest my head on his shoulder. "I like the idea of a vacation. We've been working hard."

"So hard. Need to make sure we play hard too."

"I like that even more."

Slater thumps Craig on the shoulder. "For tomorrow's trip to the hospital with the foundation, are you sure you want

Noah and me dressed as the hero and villain from our book instead of other superhero characters?"

"Definitely. I think the kids will enjoy it. They loved the book with them as the heroes."

Eyes twinkling, Noah picks up his discarded cup of tea. "I don't know how I get cast in the villain costumes when we do this. I think I'm a good guy."

"The *best* guy." Slater presses his hand to the center of Noah's chest, over his heart. At that spot beneath his shirt, is a heart tattoo with the couple's initials. I saw it a few times when he took his shirt off while I stayed with them. Noah got it as a grand gesture, public acknowledgement of his relationship and feelings for Slater, and thanks to the cameras recording post-game interviews while the players are halfway out of their gear, that tattoo is one of the most well known in the hockey world. "You're definitely superhero material."

They're sweet, gazing at each other with so much love. And when I look over at Craig and catch the curve of his gorgeous mouth as he gazes at me, like I'm the center of his world, I know anyone who sees us can feel our love. I wiggle my eyebrows at him and blow him a kiss. "I'm looking forward to being the Joker to your Batman again."

"I wanted to be Batman for sentimental reasons." Craig grabs me by the waist and tugs me to him. "I met you dressed as him a year ago, and you changed my life."

The image of Craig in the costume and then the two of us in the Batmobile flash into my mind. "Things like meeting you and driving in that tricked out car didn't happen to me. Not until you. Now, I never know what's coming, but I know we'll ride through it together." With a heady rush of anticipation for our future, I link my arms around his neck. "I love you."

Craig smiles and brushes his finger along my cheek.

"Love you, too. You crashed into my life, into my heart, and every day you make me feel like I can do anything, because I have you by my side. You say I'm your superhero, and Ty, you're definitely mine."

"You always make me feel like one. Super fans of each other, superheroes to each other, whatever the label, I'll take it. And I'll take you. Forever." My body buzzing and my heart full, I pull him for a kiss.

Thank you for reading Ty and Craig's story! If you enjoyed it, I would be so grateful if you would leave a review. Reviews, even one line long, help other readers find my books.

For Slater and Noah's romance (Ty makes an appearance!), check out *Scoring Slater*, part of the Pride of the Bedlam series. It's also part of the multi-author Hockey Allies Bachelor Bid series.

Here's the blurb:

Slater Knox is known around the league as the tough enforcer for the Buffalo Bedlam. His popular social media accounts and open relationship with the fans have made him one of the most beloved players in hockey. They've also earned him a spot in the All-Star game, and an invitation to be a bachelor at a charity auction. For all his living in the spotlight, he's hiding a secret... He's in love with his best friend and keeping quiet grows harder each day.

Noah Alzado is the newest addition to the team, and has spent the last few months joined at the hip with his best friend Slater. Slater is everything Noah wants, but won't let himself have. They are best friends, roommates, and teammates, that's three complications too many. Plus, Noah guards his private life as fiercely as Slater shares his own. His best option is to keep his head down, help his team win, and not do anything stupid... like kissing Slater again.

Everything comes to a head during All-Star weekend, where the best in the league compete for ultimate bragging rights, and at the auction, where temptation is hot enough to melt the ice. The chemistry between Slater and Noah is scorching, but can they lower their defenses enough to make a play for love?

Read Scoring Slater today:
   https://www.susanscottshelley.com/pride-of-the-bedlam

ACKNOWLEDGMENTS

Thank you to Chantal Mer and Tina Cambria for being amazing critique partners, beta readers, and friends.

Thank you to my proofreader, Nikki S.

I also have to thank my husband, who is my very own superhero.

And finally, thank you to my readers!

ABOUT THE AUTHOR

USA TODAY bestselling author Susan Scott Shelley writes romance with heat and heart that celebrates love without limits. She enjoys watching hockey, training for her next run, reading romance novels, and binging episodes of her favorite British TV shows. Susan lives in Philadelphia with her husband and also works as a professional voice over artist. A city girl who likes being out in nature as often as possible, she has yet to meet a plant she hasn't wanted to take home and she really wants a pet crow.

Visit her website for her book list, reader newsletter, ways to connect, and more: https://susanscottshelley.com.

ALSO BY SUSAN SCOTT SHELLEY

<u>The Games We Play series</u>

Power Move

<u>The Philadelphia Frenzy series</u>

Mad Scramble, Hometown Hero, Team Spirit

<u>The Falling series</u>

Falling Faster

Hold on Forever (related to the series)

<u>Bliss Bakery series</u>

Sugar Crush, Heart of the Batter

<u>Pride of the Bedlam series</u>

Skating on Chance, Holding on Tight, Scoring Slater

Playing with Pride (series collection)

<u>Philadelphia Power series</u>

Against the Rush, Over the Top, Behind the Mask, From the First

Powered by Love (series collection)

<u>Love & Rugby series</u>

Spiral, Spark, Smolder, Shine, Surprise, Swoon

Love & Rugby, vol. 1, Love & Rugby, vol. 2,

Love & Rugby, the Complete Collection

<u>Love & Rugby: Season of Love</u>

Savor, Seduce, Stay

Love & Rugby: Season of Love, the Complete Collection

<u>Buffalo Bedlam series</u>

Making His Move, Fighting For More, Taking His Shot

Playing to Win (series collection)

<u>Rocked by Love series</u>

Love Notes, Love Song

<u>Game of Love series</u>

Rekindled, Captivated, Enamored

Game of Love (series collection)

<u>Holiday Hearts series</u>

Kiss Me Again, More Than Words, All I Want, Marry Me

Holiday Hearts (series collection)

<u>Other Novellas</u>

Flirting on Ice, Simmering Ice, Tackled by the Girl Next Door

Sign up for Susan's reader newsletter:

https://susanscottshelley.com/newsletter

www.ingramcontent.com/pod-product-compliance
Ingram Content Group UK Ltd.
Pitfield, Milton Keynes, MK11 3LW, UK
UKHW030731240225
455493UK00005B/373